D1220979

AGATHA CHRISTIE

Hah!
Note the name
of the Rowboat on
p.19!! ABW III 1 April, 2016

EVIL UNDER THE SUN

ADAPTED BY **DIDIER** QUELLA-GUYOT

ILLUSTRATED BY **THIERRY** JOLLET

HARPER

Thank you to my brother for the photos.
A thousand thanks to my wife and my daughter for their support and their love.
I dedicate this book to the memory of my father, who passed over to the other side
while we were working on this book.
— Thierry Jollet

HARPER
An imprint of HarperCollins*Publishers*
77-85 Fulham Palace Road
Hammersmith, London W6 8JB
www.harpercollins.co.uk

First published by HARPER 2013
1

Comic book edition published in France as *Les Vacances d'Hercule Poirot*
© 2012 Heupé SARL / Emmanuel Proust Éditions,
55, rue Traversière, 75012 Paris. www.epeditions.com
Based on *Evil Under the Sun* © 1941 by Agatha Christie Limited. All rights reserved.
Agatha Christie®, Poirot® copyright © 2010 Agatha Christie Ltd.
www.agathachristie.com

Adapted by Didier Quella-Guyot.
Illustrated by Thierry Jollet.
Colour by Christophe Bouchard.
English edition edited by David Brawn.

ISBN 978-0-00-745134-0

Printed and bound in China by South China Printing Company Ltd.

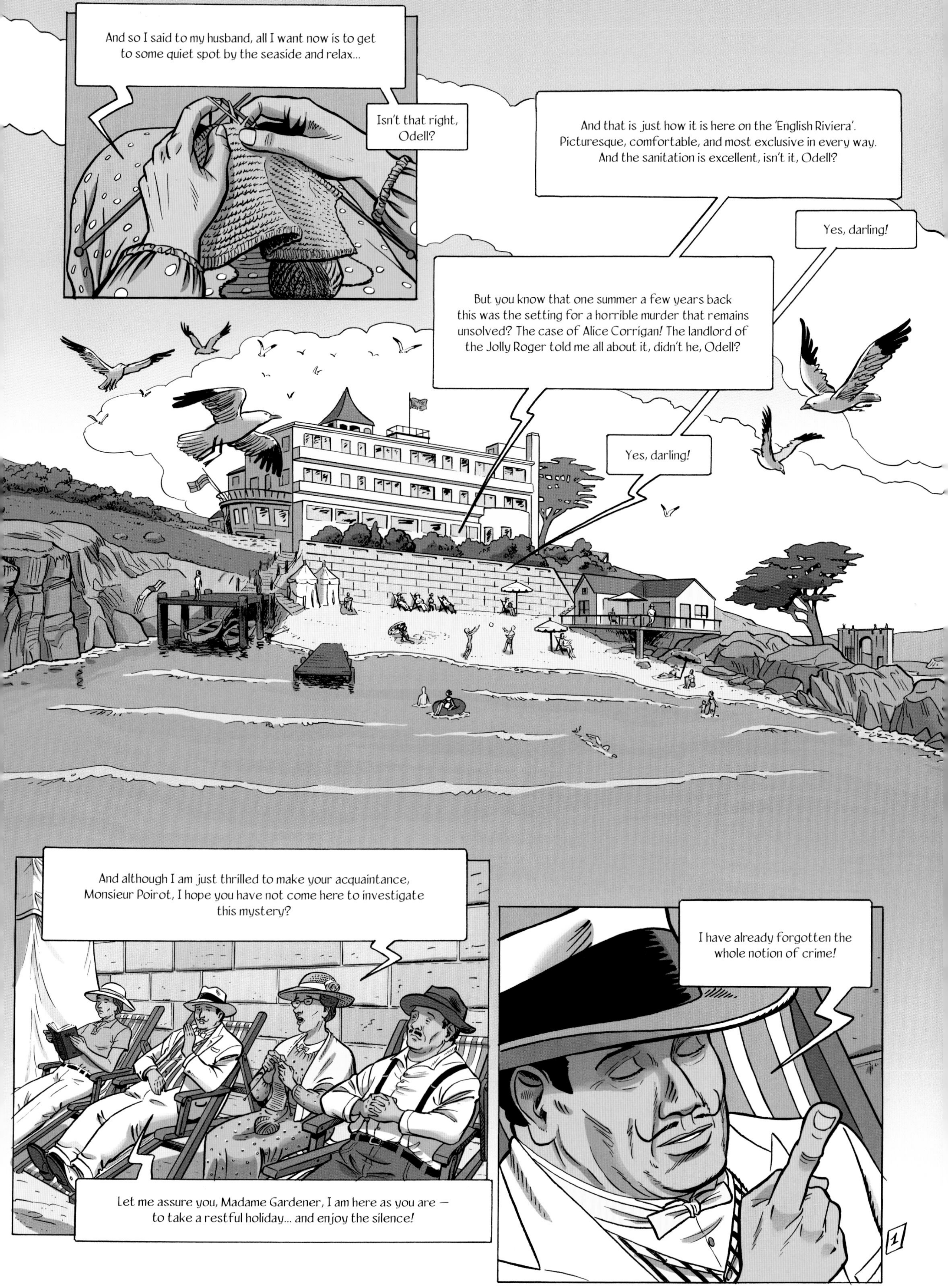

And so I said to my husband, all I want now is to get to some quiet spot by the seaside and relax...
Isn't that right, Odell?
And that is just how it is here on the 'English Riviera'. Picturesque, comfortable, and most exclusive in every way. And the sanitation is excellent, isn't it, Odell?
Yes, darling!
But you know that one summer a few years back this was the setting for a horrible murder that remains unsolved? The case of Alice Corrigan! The landlord of the Jolly Roger told me all about it, didn't he, Odell?
Yes, darling!
And although I am just thrilled to make your acquaintance, Monsieur Poirot, I hope you have not come here to investigate this mystery?
Let me assure you, Madame Gardener, I am here as you are — to take a restful holiday... and enjoy the silence!
I have already forgotten the whole notion of crime!

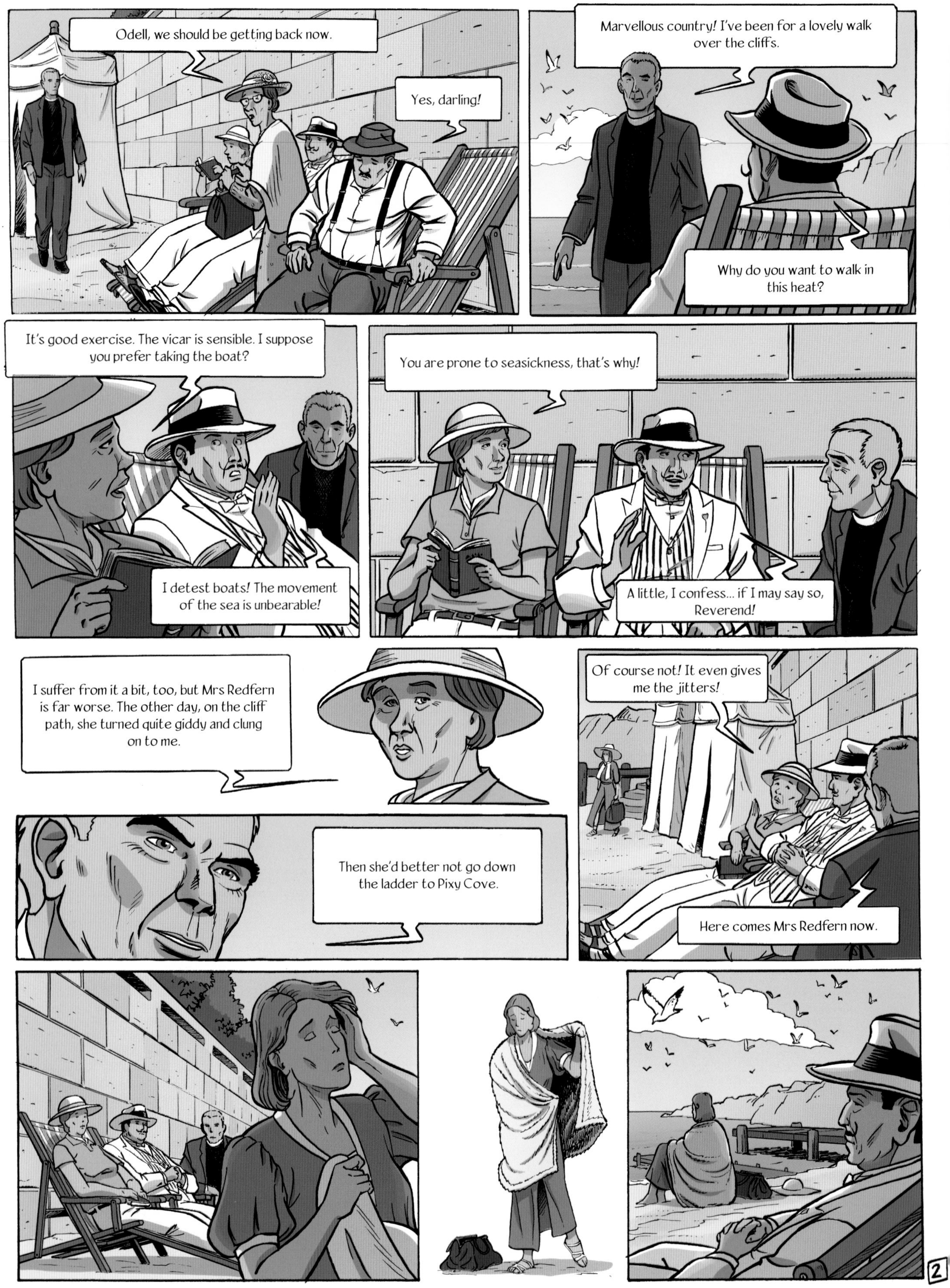
Odell, we should be getting back now.
Yes, darling!
Marvellous country! I've been for a lovely walk over the cliffs.
Why do you want to walk in this heat?
It's good exercise. The vicar is sensible. I suppose you prefer taking the boat?
I detest boats! The movement of the sea is unbearable!
You are prone to seasickness, that's why!
A little, I confess... if I may say so, Reverend!
I suffer from it a bit, too, but Mrs Redfern is far worse. The other day, on the cliff path, she turned quite giddy and clung on to me.
Of course not! It even gives me the jitters!
Then she'd better not go down the ladder to Pixy Cove.
Here comes Mrs Redfern now.
2

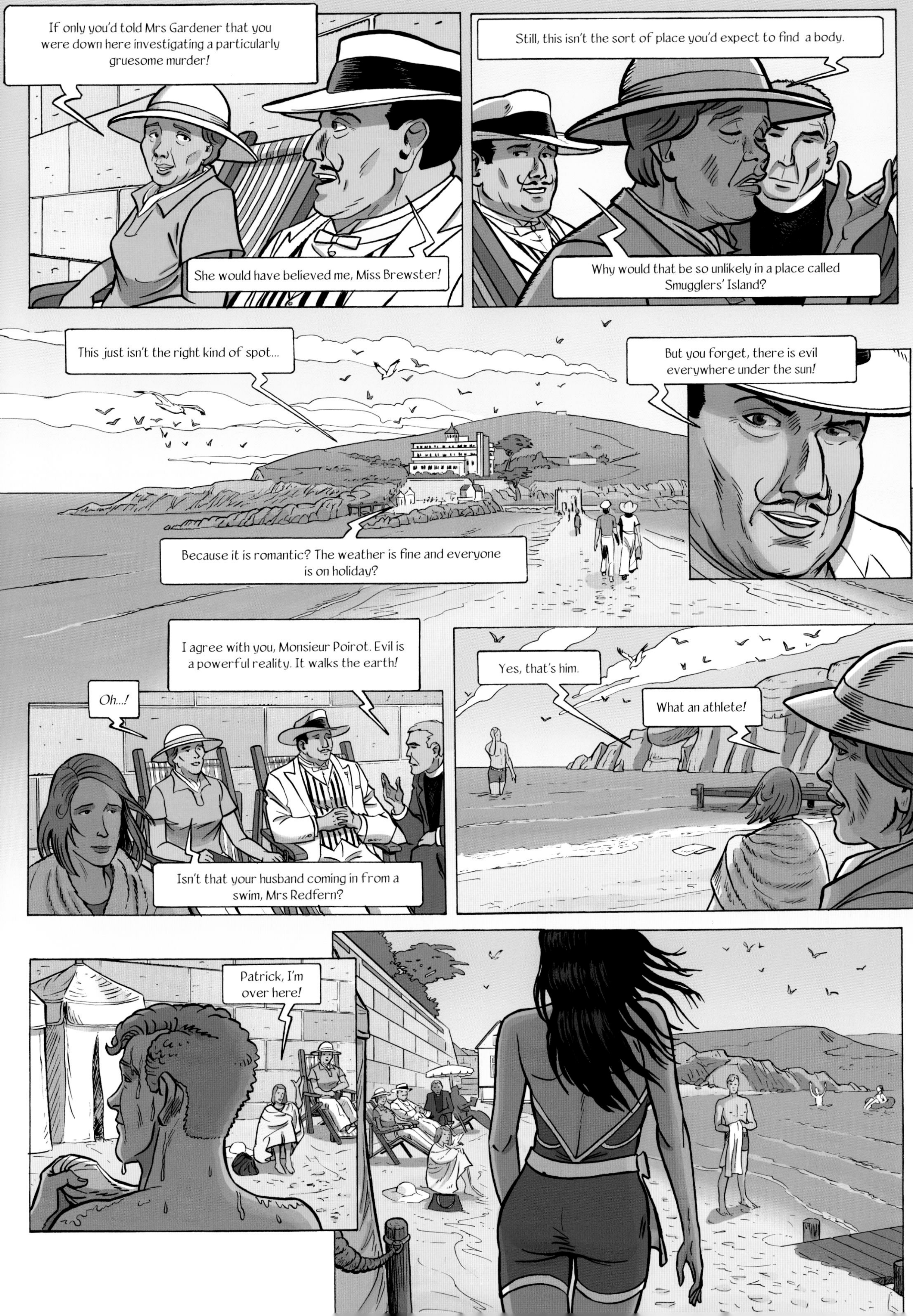
If only you'd told Mrs Gardener that you were down here investigating a particularly gruesome murder!
She would have believed me, Miss Brewster!
Still, this isn't the sort of place you'd expect to find a body.
Why would that be so unlikely in a place called Smugglers' Island?
This just isn't the right kind of spot...
Because it is romantic? The weather is fine and everyone is on holiday?
But you forget, there is evil everywhere under the sun!
I agree with you, Monsieur Poirot. Evil is a powerful reality. It walks the earth!
Oh...!
Isn't that your husband coming in from a swim, Mrs Redfern?
Yes, that's him.
What an athlete!
Patrick, I'm over here!

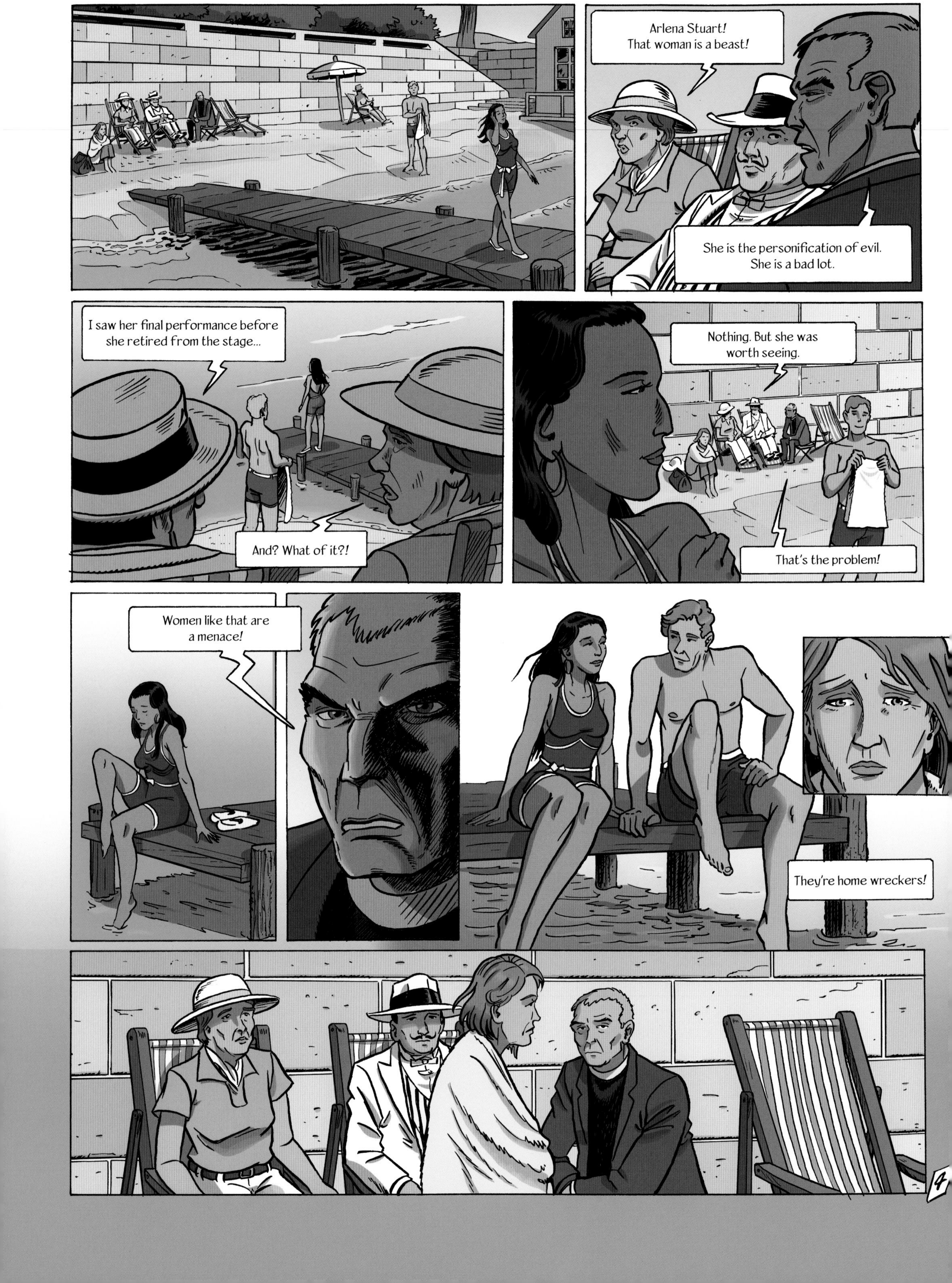
Arlena Stuart! That woman is a beast!
She is the personification of evil. She is a bad lot.
I saw her final performance before she retired from the stage...
And? What of it?!
Nothing. But she was worth seeing.
That's the problem!
Women like that are a menace!
They're home wreckers!

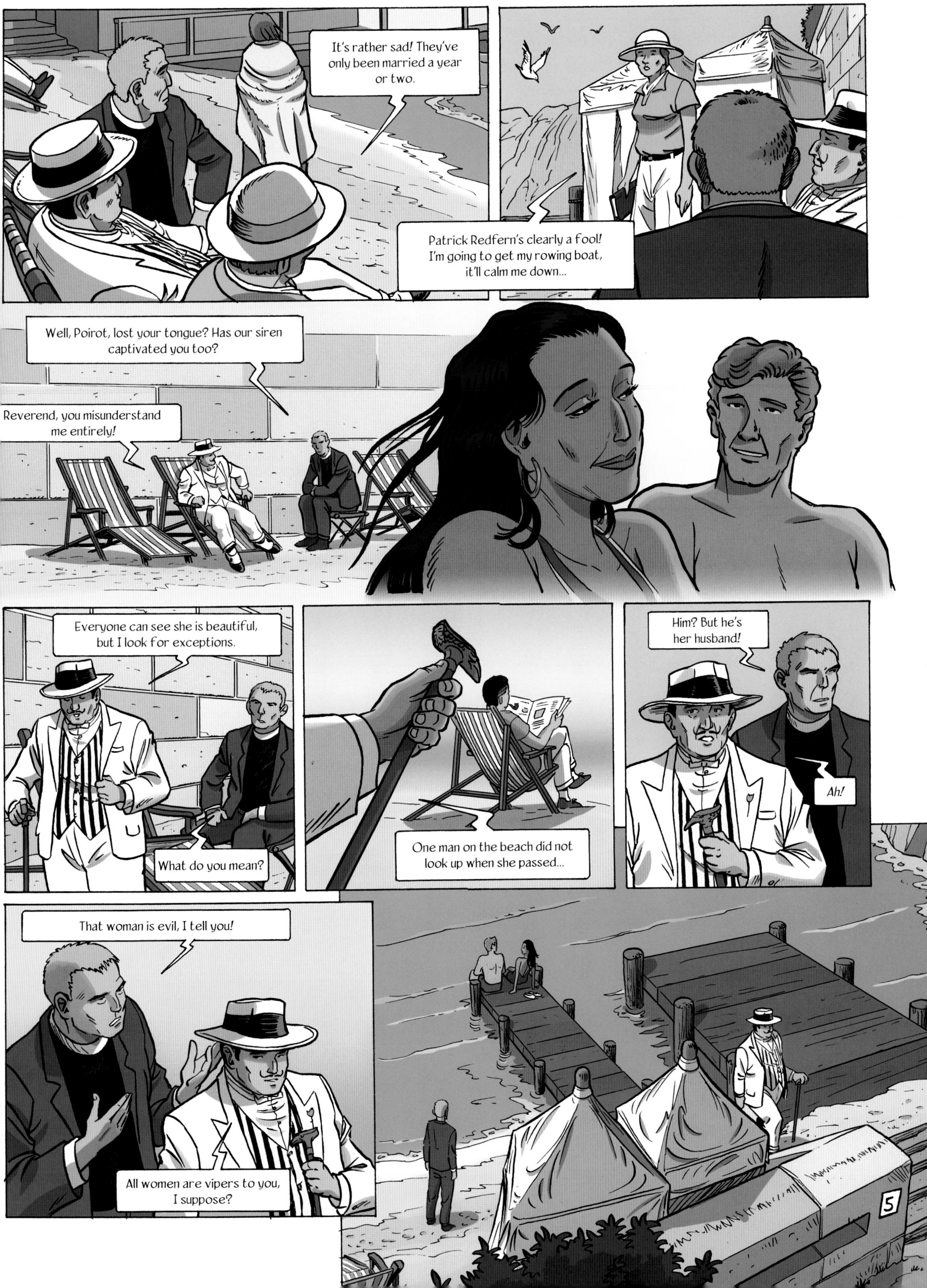

It's rather sad! They've only been married a year or two.
Patrick Redfern's clearly a fool! I'm going to get my rowing boat, it'll calm me down...
Well, Poirot, lost your tongue? Has our siren captivated you too?
Reverend, you misunderstand me entirely!
Everyone can see she is beautiful, but I look for exceptions.
What do you mean?
One man on the beach did not look up when she passed...
Him? But he's her husband!
Ah!
That woman is evil, I tell you!
All women are vipers to you, I suppose?

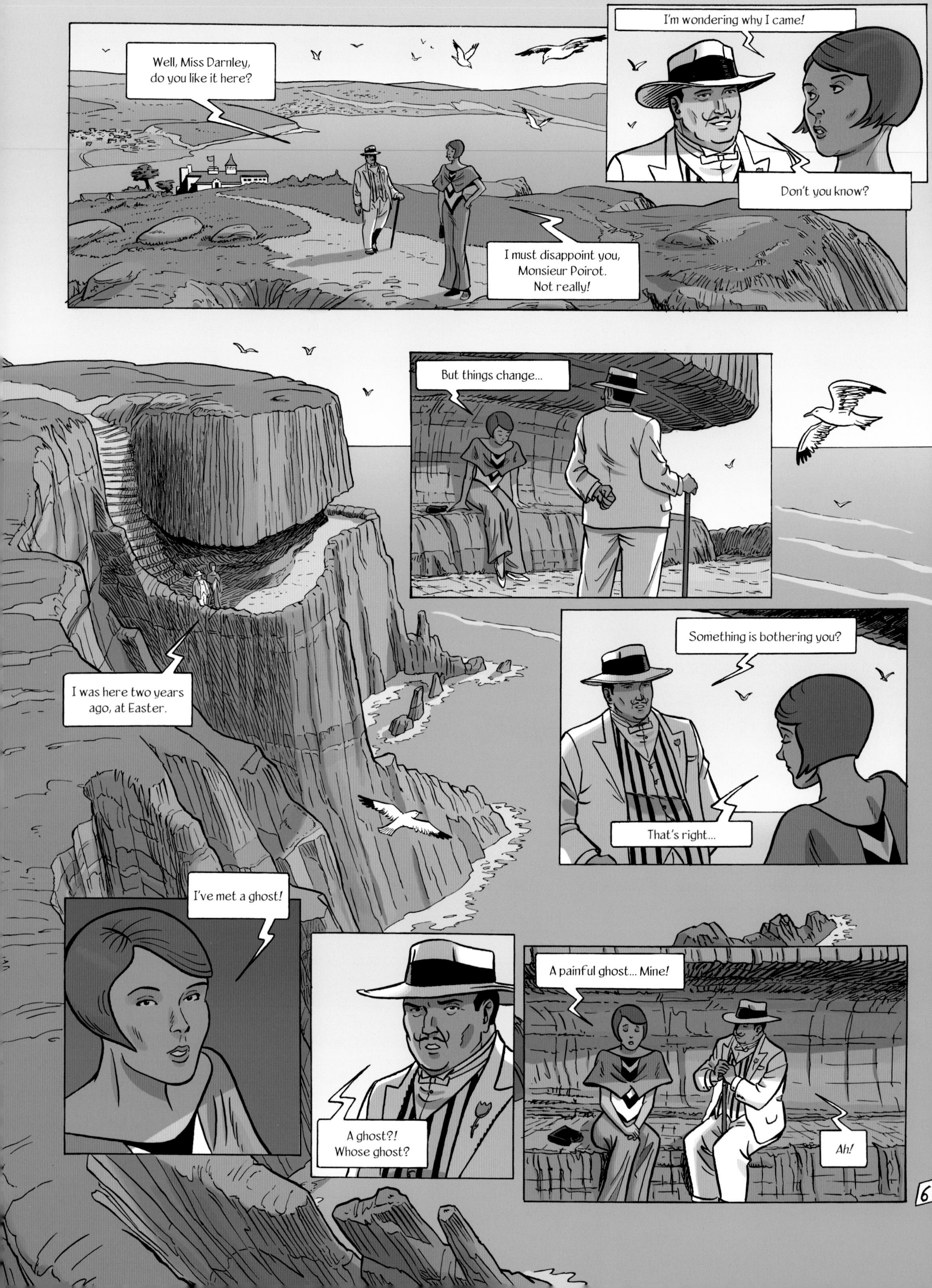

Well, Miss Darnley, do you like it here?
I must disappoint you, Monsieur Poirot. Not really!
I'm wondering why I came!
Don't you know?
I was here two years ago, at Easter.
But things change...
Something is bothering you?
That's right...
I've met a ghost!
A ghost?! Whose ghost?
A painful ghost... Mine!
Ah!

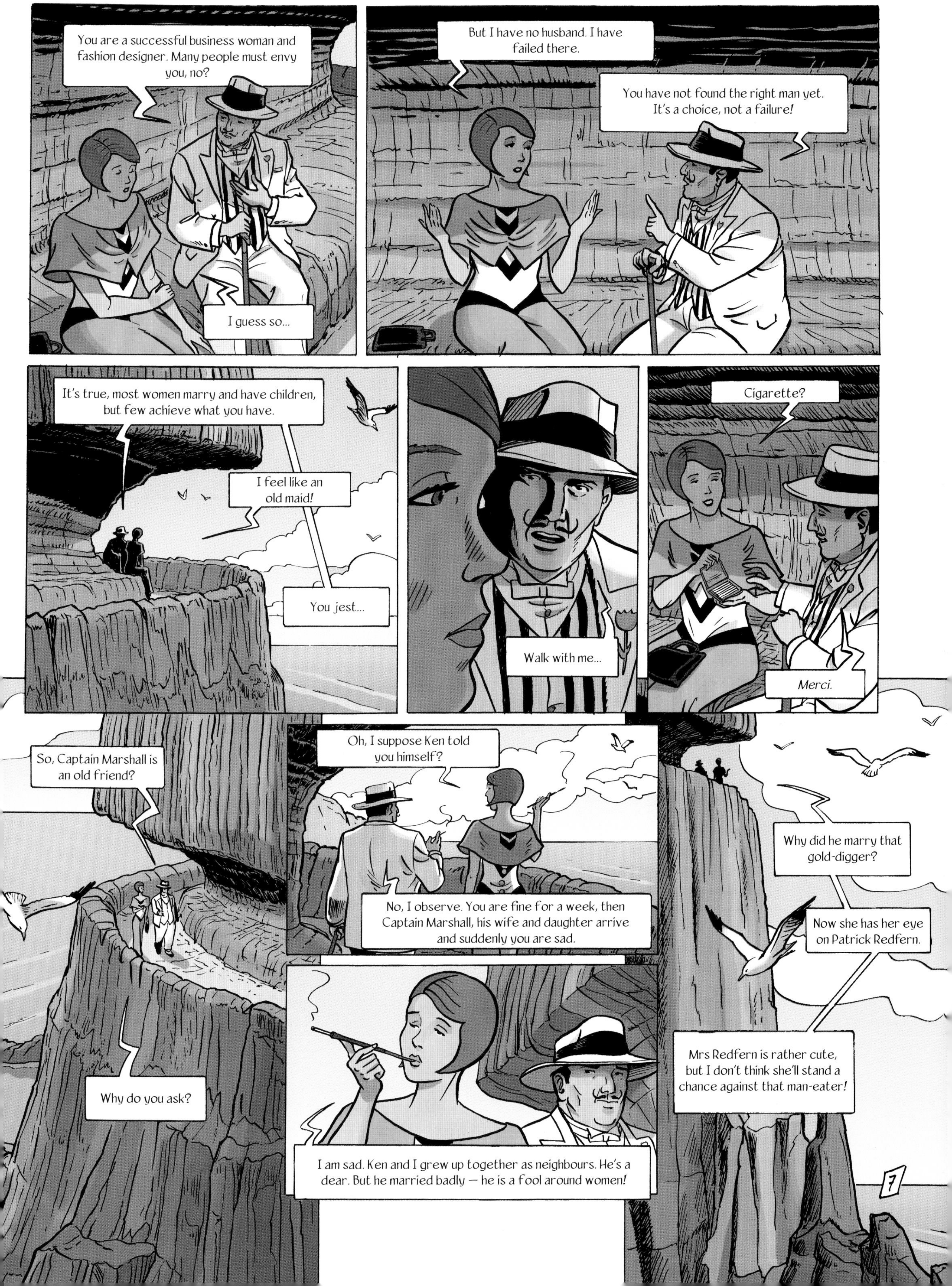
You are a successful business woman and fashion designer. Many people must envy you, no?
I guess so...
But I have no husband. I have failed there.
You have not found the right man yet. It's a choice, not a failure!
It's true, most women marry and have children, but few achieve what you have.
I feel like an old maid!
You jest...
Walk with me...
Cigarette?
Merci.
So, Captain Marshall is an old friend?
Why do you ask?
Oh, I suppose Ken told you himself?
No, I observe. You are fine for a week, then Captain Marshall, his wife and daughter arrive and suddenly you are sad.
I am sad. Ken and I grew up together as neighbours. He's a dear. But he married badly – he is a fool around women!
Why did he marry that gold-digger?
Now she has her eye on Patrick Redfern.
Mrs Redfern is rather cute, but I don't think she'll stand a chance against that man-eater!

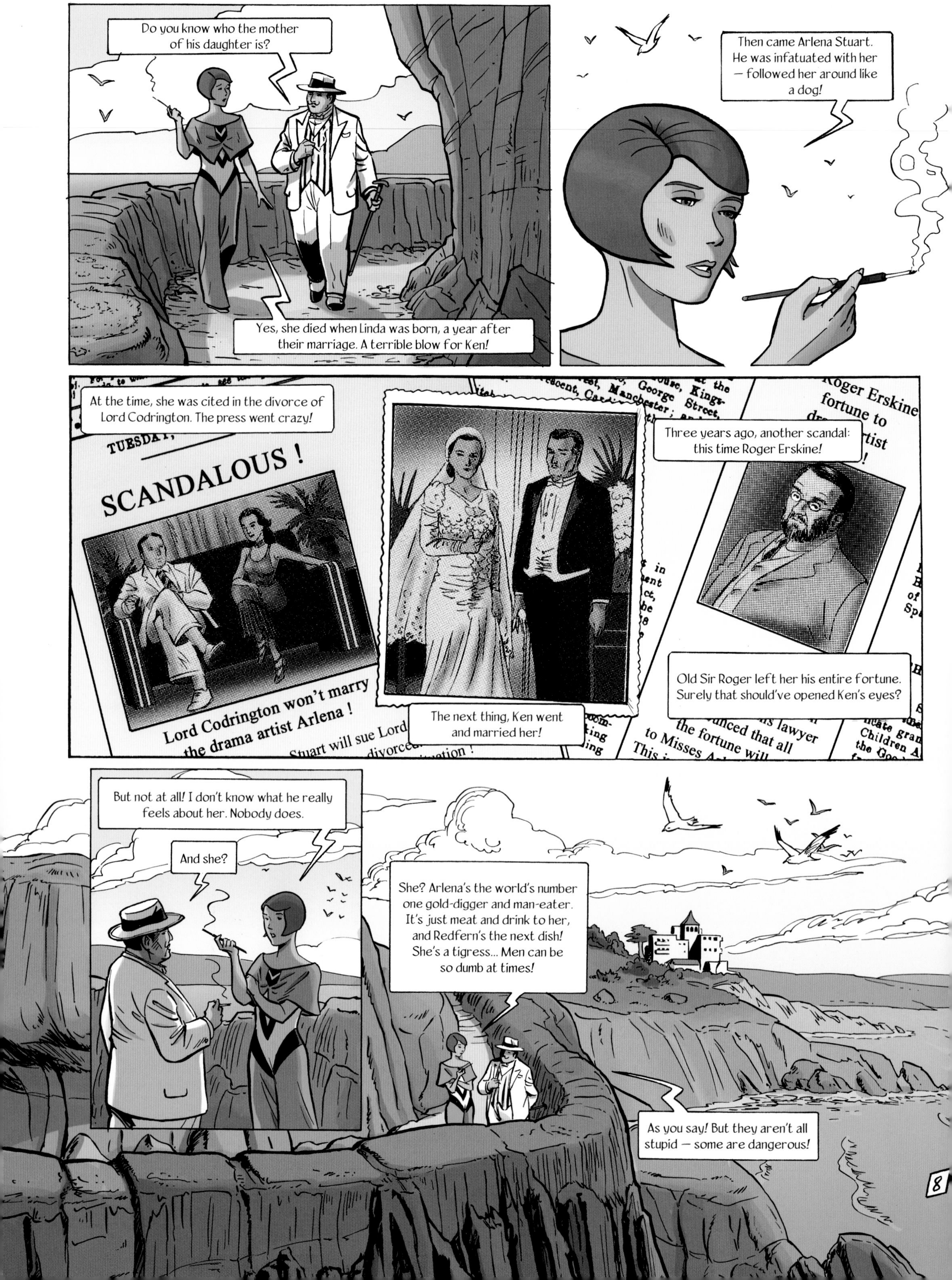

Do you know who the mother of his daughter is?
Yes, she died when Linda was born, a year after their marriage. A terrible blow for Ken!
Then came Arlena Stuart. He was infatuated with her — followed her around like a dog!
At the time, she was cited in the divorce of Lord Codrington. The press went crazy!
TUESDAY,
SCANDALOUS !
Lord Codrington won't marry
the drama artist Arlena !
The next thing, Ken went and married her!
Roger Erskine
Three years ago, another scandal: this time Roger Erskine!
Old Sir Roger left her his entire fortune. Surely that should've opened Ken's eyes?
But not at all! I don't know what he really feels about her. Nobody does.
And she?
She? Arlena's the world's number one gold-digger and man-eater. It's just meat and drink to her, and Redfern's the next dish! She's a tigress... Men can be so dumb at times!
As you say! But they aren't all stupid — some are dangerous!

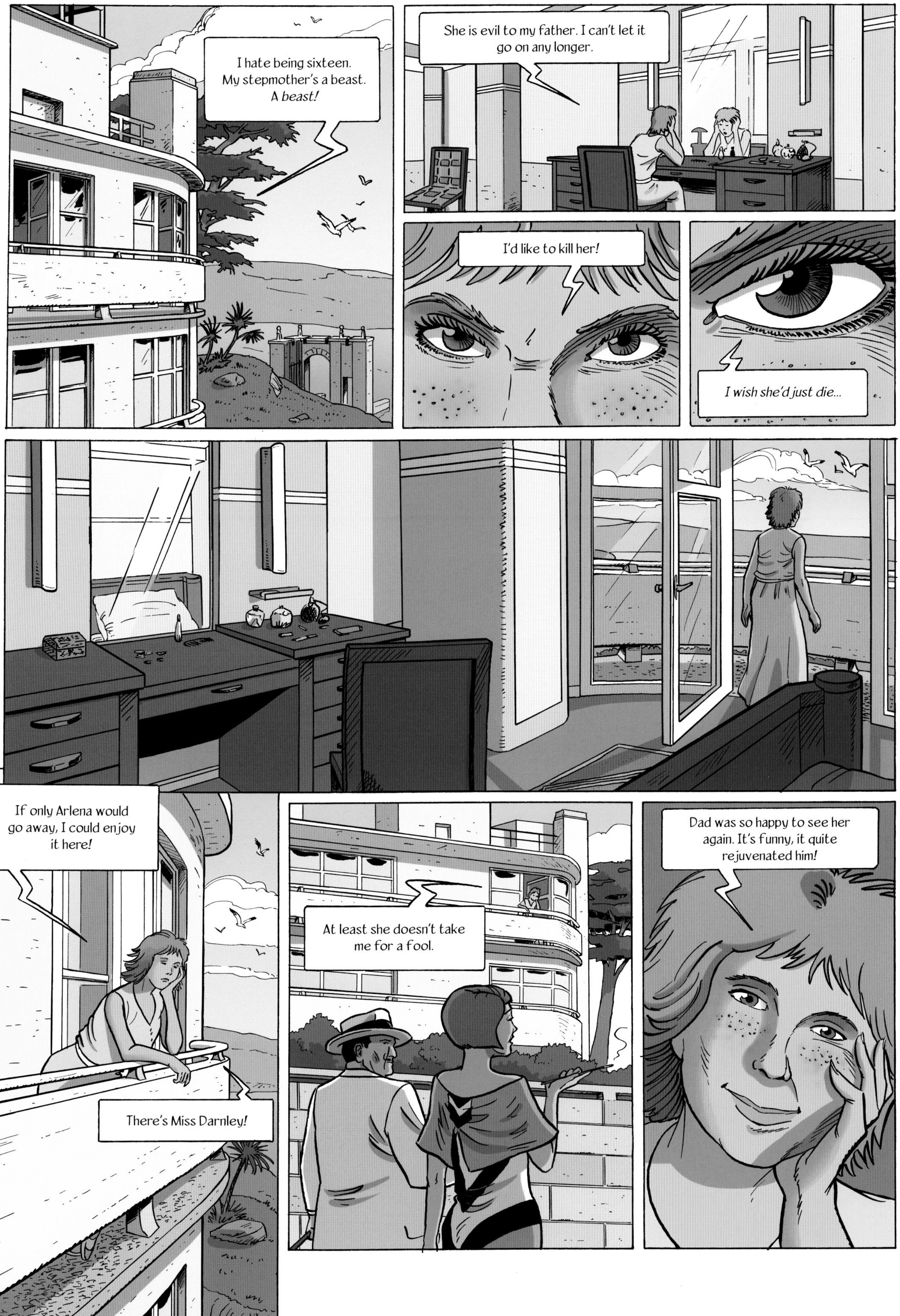
I hate being sixteen. My stepmother's a beast. A *beast!*
She is evil to my father. I can't let it go on any longer.
I'd like to kill her!
I wish she'd just die...
If only Arlena would go away, I could enjoy it here!
There's Miss Darnley!
At least she doesn't take me for a fool.
Dad was so happy to see her again. It's funny, it quite rejuvenated him!

Yes?

Oh, it's you, Ken!

I came to see if you were ready...

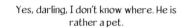

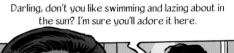

Arlena?

Yes?

Redfern, have you met him before?

Yes, darling, I don't know where. He is rather a pet.

That's what I thought.

Did you know he'd be here?

Oh no, darling! It was the *greatest* surprise!

You were very keen we should come here...

Darling, don't you like swimming and lazing about in the sun? I'm sure you'll adore it here.

I can see that you intend to enjoy yourself!

Don't be horrid! They're a nice young couple and that boy's fond of his wife. You know I can't help it if people are crazy about me...

The one thing I do know, Arlena, is that I know you only too well!

10

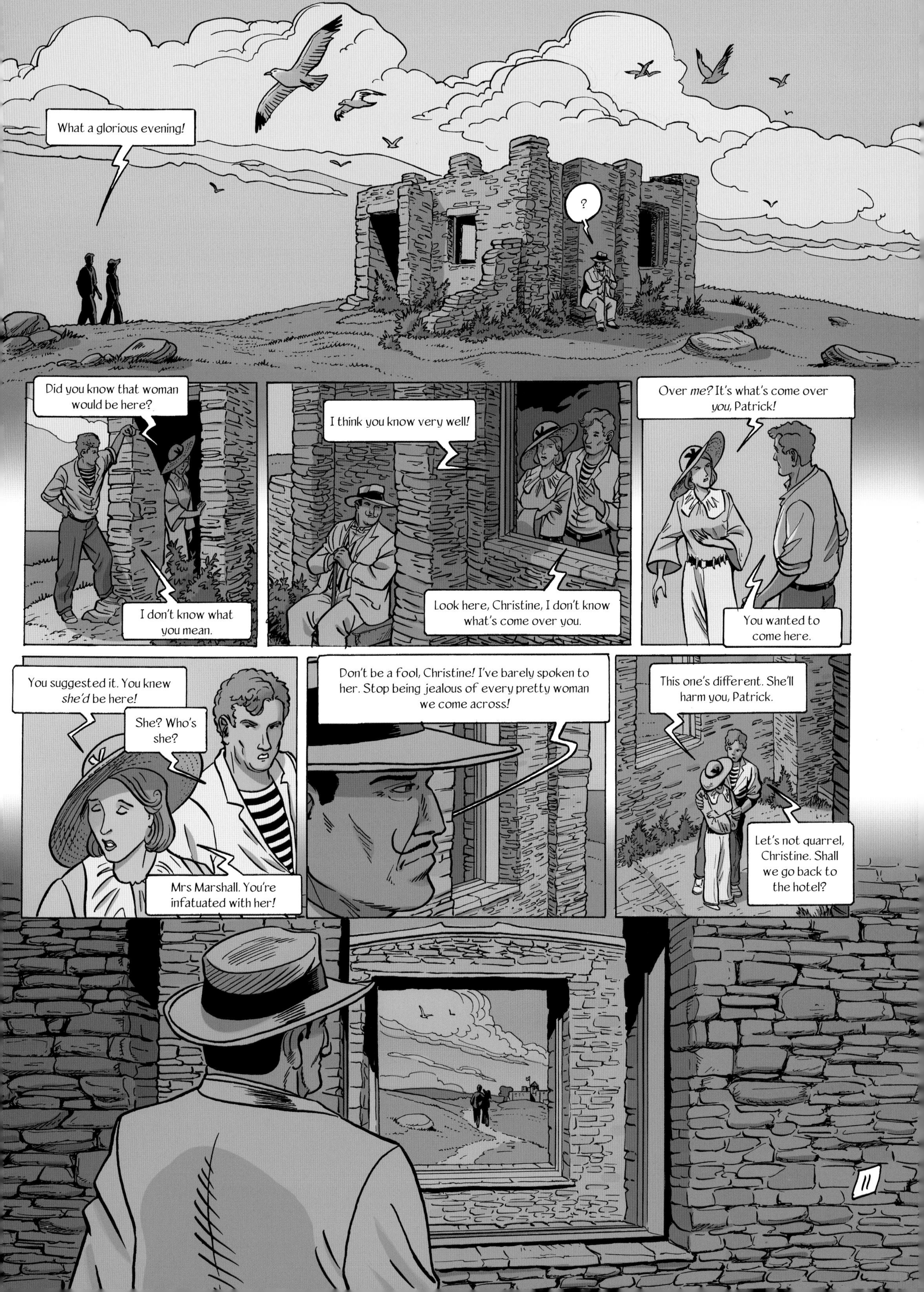
What a glorious evening!
?
Did you know that woman would be here?
I don't know what you mean.
I think you know very well!
Look here, Christine, I don't know what's come over you.
Over *me*? It's what's come over *you*, Patrick!
You wanted to come here.
You suggested it. You knew *she'd* be here!
She? Who's she?
Mrs Marshall. You're infatuated with her!
Don't be a fool, Christine! I've barely spoken to her. Stop being jealous of every pretty woman we come across!
This one's different. She'll harm you, Patrick.
Let's not quarrel, Christine. Shall we go back to the hotel?

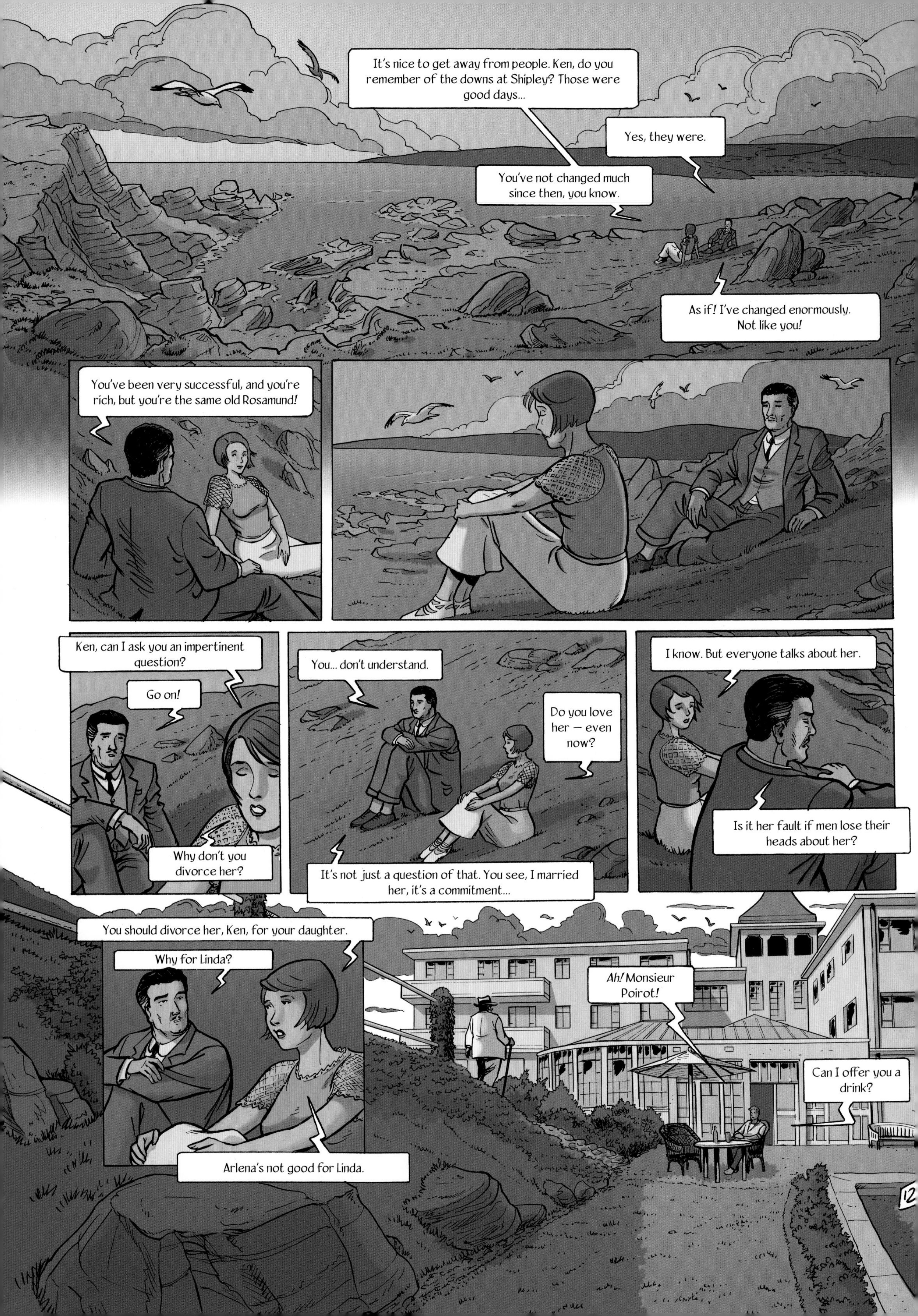
It's nice to get away from people. Ken, do you remember of the downs at Shipley? Those were good days...
Yes, they were.
You've not changed much since then, you know.
As if! I've changed enormously. Not like you!
You've been very successful, and you're rich, but you're the same old Rosamund!
Ken, can I ask you an impertinent question?
Go on!
Why don't you divorce her?
You... don't understand.
Do you love her — even now?
It's not just a question of that. You see, I married her, it's a commitment...
I know. But everyone talks about her.
Is it her fault if men lose their heads about her?
You should divorce her, Ken, for your daughter.
Why for Linda?
Arlena's not good for Linda.
Ah! Monsieur Poirot!
Can I offer you a drink?

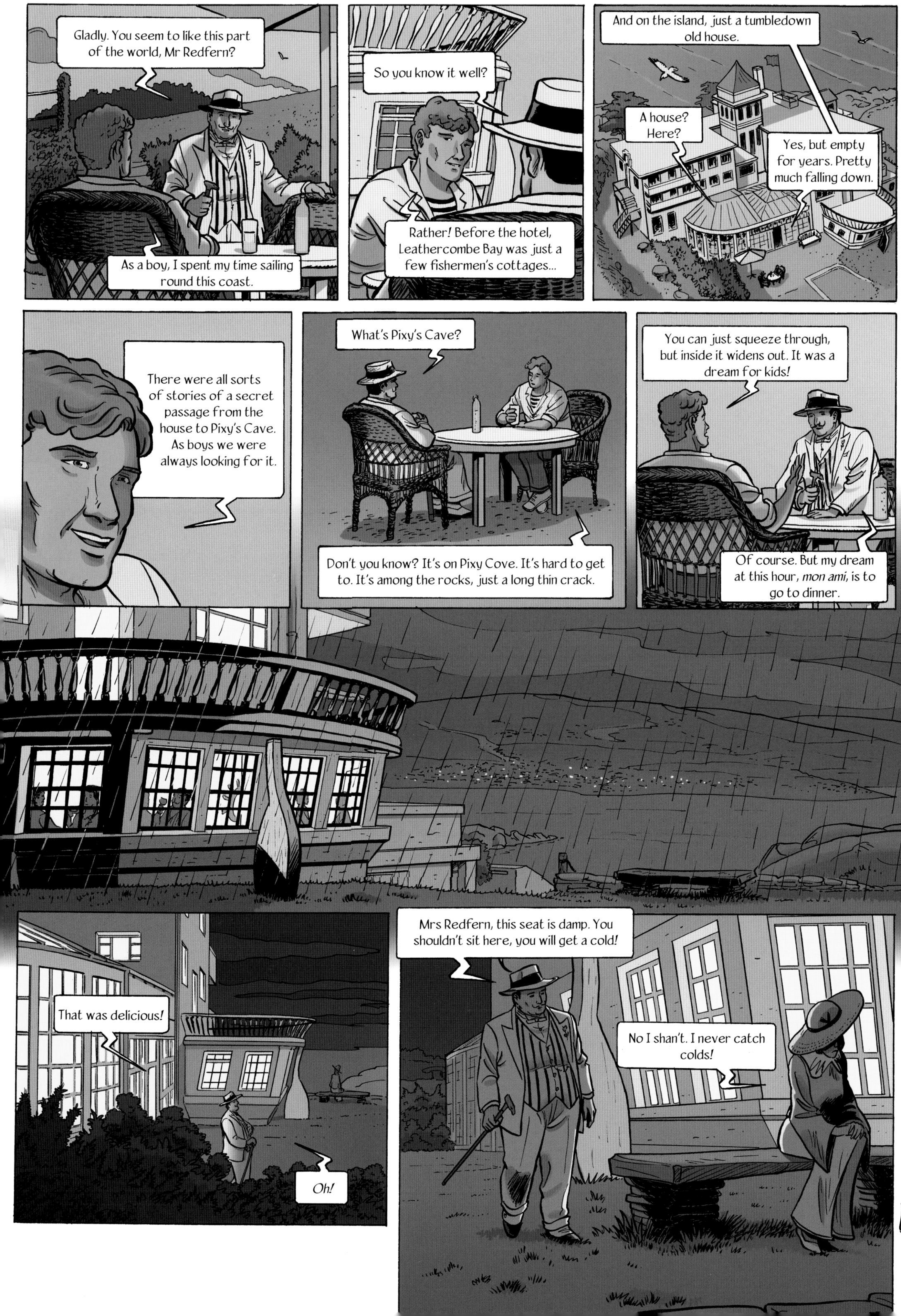

Gladly. You seem to like this part of the world, Mr Redfern?
As a boy, I spent my time sailing round this coast.
So you know it well?
Rather! Before the hotel, Leathercombe Bay was just a few fishermen's cottages...
And on the island, just a tumbledown old house.
A house? Here?
Yes, but empty for years. Pretty much falling down.
There were all sorts of stories of a secret passage from the house to Pixy's Cave. As boys we were always looking for it.
What's Pixy's Cave?
Don't you know? It's on Pixy Cove. It's hard to get to. It's among the rocks, just a long thin crack.
You can just squeeze through, but inside it widens out. It was a dream for kids!
Of course. But my dream at this hour, *mon ami*, is to go to dinner.
That was delicious!
Oh!
Mrs Redfern, this seat is damp. You shouldn't sit here, you will get a cold!
No I shan't. I never catch colds!

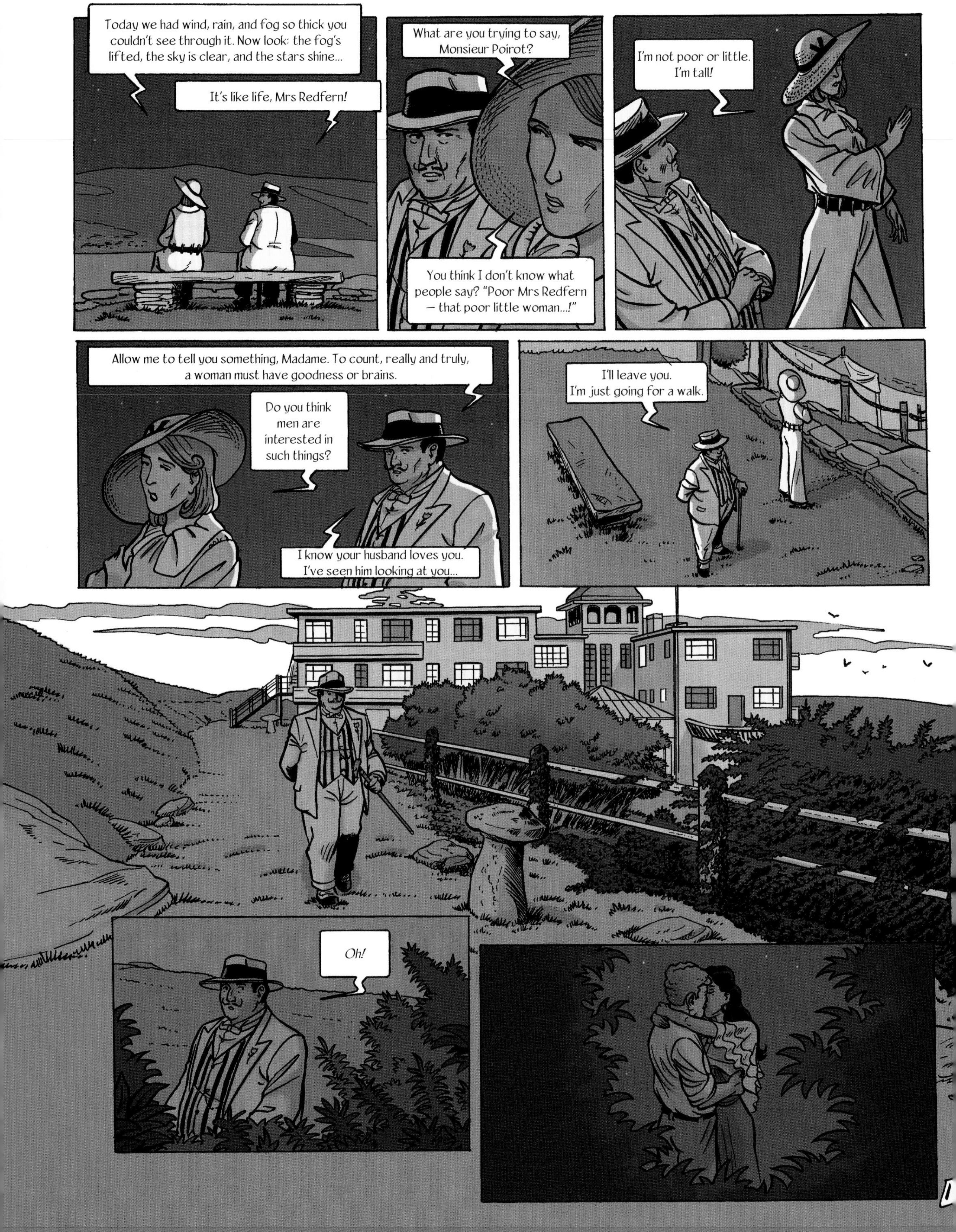
Today we had wind, rain, and fog so thick you couldn't see through it. Now look: the fog's lifted, the sky is clear, and the stars shine...
It's like life, Mrs Redfern!
What are you trying to say, Monsieur Poirot?
You think I don't know what people say? "Poor Mrs Redfern — that poor little woman...!"
I'm not poor or little. I'm tall!
Allow me to tell you something, Madame. To count, really and truly, a woman must have goodness or brains.
Do you think men are interested in such things?
I know your husband loves you. I've seen him looking at you...
I'll leave you. I'm just going for a walk.
Oh!

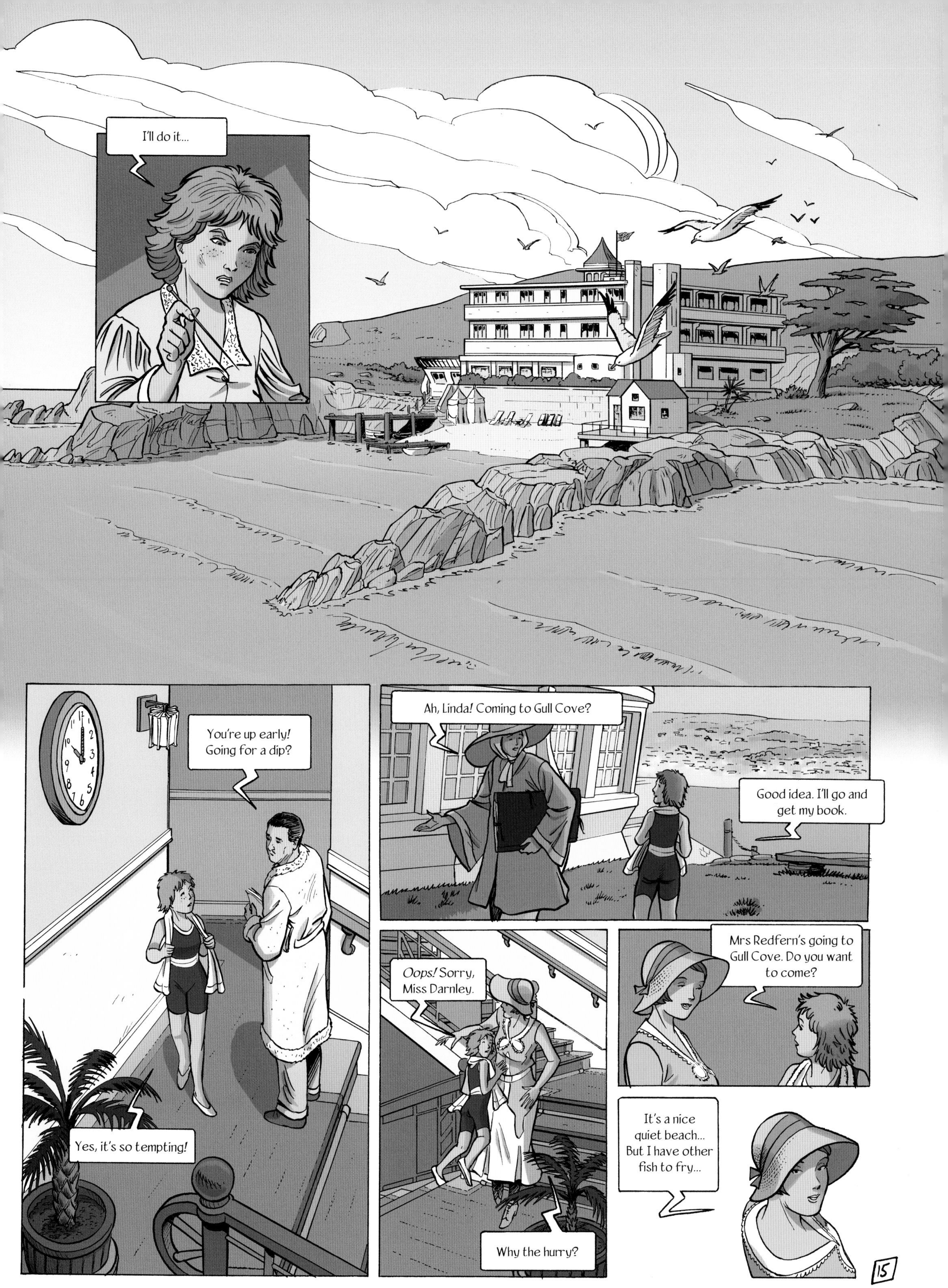
I'll do it...
You're up early! Going for a dip?
Yes, it's so tempting!
Ah, Linda! Coming to Gull Cove?
Good idea. I'll go and get my book.
Oops! Sorry, Miss Darnley.
Why the hurry?
Mrs Redfern's going to Gull Cove. Do you want to come?
It's a nice quiet beach... But I have other fish to fry...
15

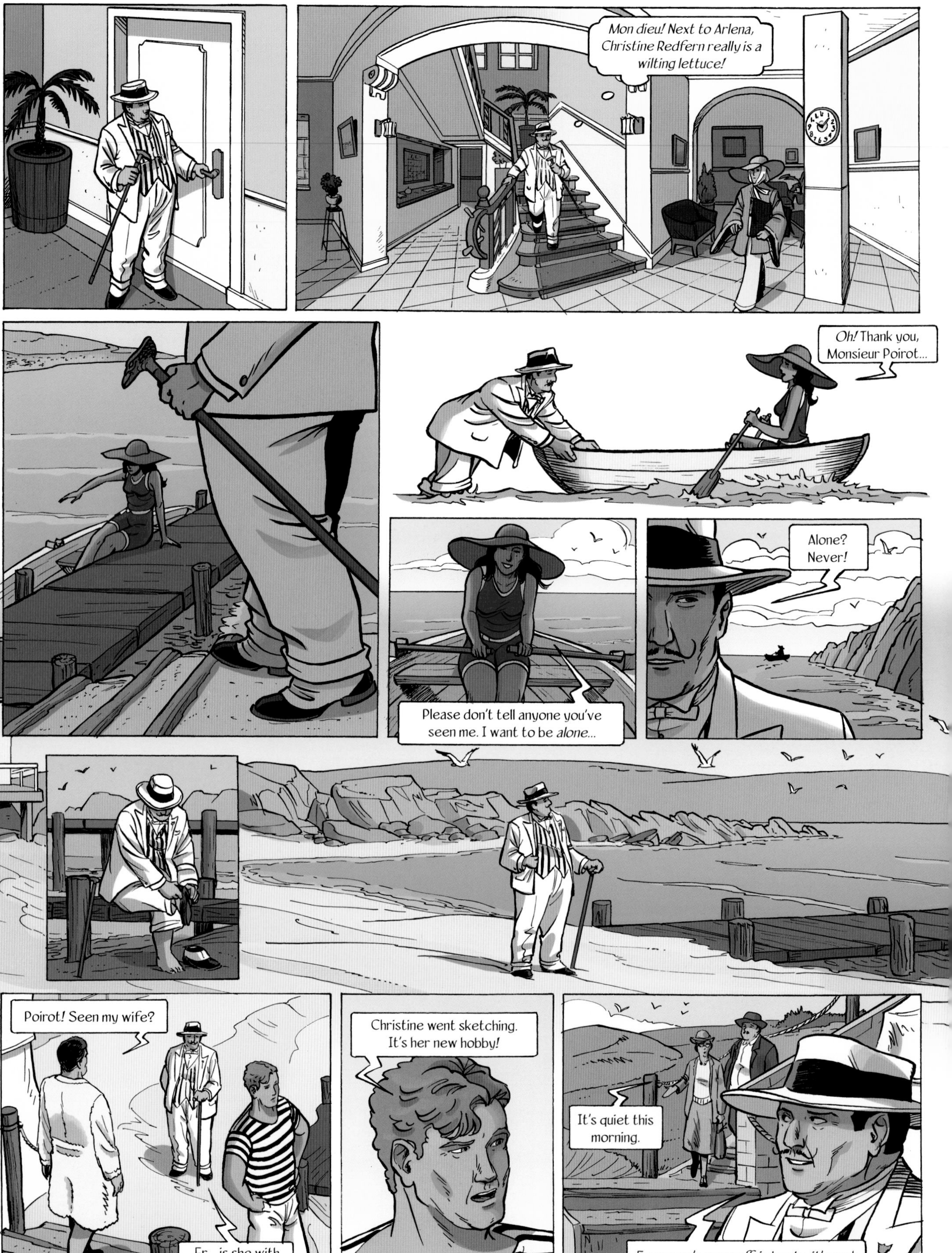

Mon dieu! Next to Arlena, Christine Redfern really is a wilting lettuce!
Oh! Thank you, Monsieur Poirot...
Please don't tell anyone you've seen me. I want to be *alone*...
Alone? Never!
Poirot! Seen my wife?
Er... is she with Madame Redfern?
Christine went sketching. It's her new hobby!
It's quiet this morning.
Everyone's gone off in boats, it's such a beautiful day...

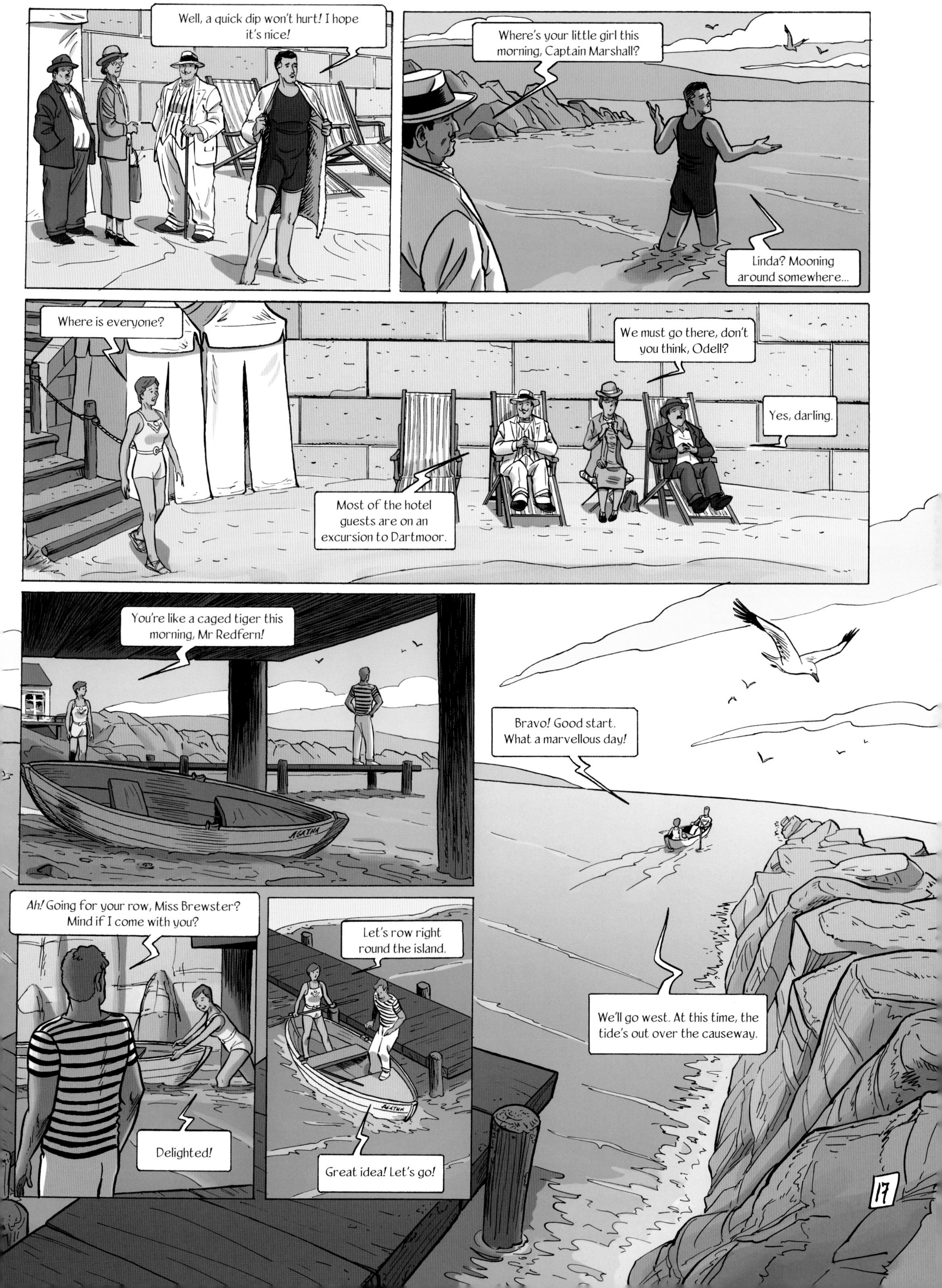
Well, a quick dip won't hurt! I hope it's nice!
Where's your little girl this morning, Captain Marshall?
Linda? Mooning around somewhere...
Where is everyone?
We must go there, don't you think, Odell?
Yes, darling.
Most of the hotel guests are on an excursion to Dartmoor.
You're like a caged tiger this morning, Mr Redfern!
AGATHA
Ah! Going for your row, Miss Brewster? Mind if I come with you?
Delighted!
Let's row right round the island.
Great idea! Let's go!
Bravo! Good start. What a marvellous day!
We'll go west. At this time, the tide's out over the causeway.

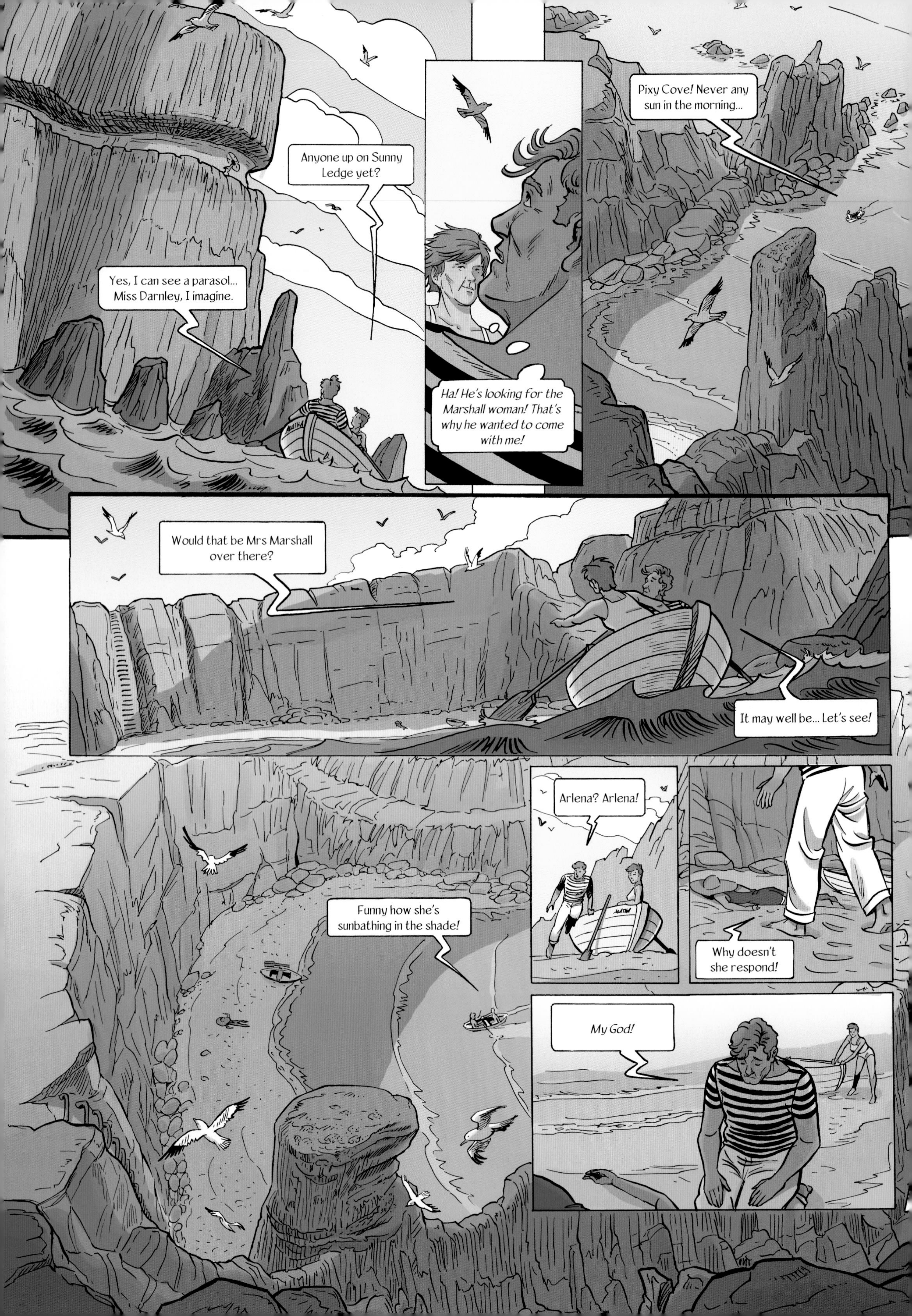
Anyone up on Sunny Ledge yet?
Yes, I can see a parasol... Miss Darnley, I imagine.
Ha! He's looking for the Marshall woman! That's why he wanted to come with me!
Pixy Cove! Never any sun in the morning...
Would that be Mrs Marshall over there?
It may well be... Let's see!
Funny how she's sunbathing in the shade!
Arlena? Arlena!
Why doesn't she respond!
My God!

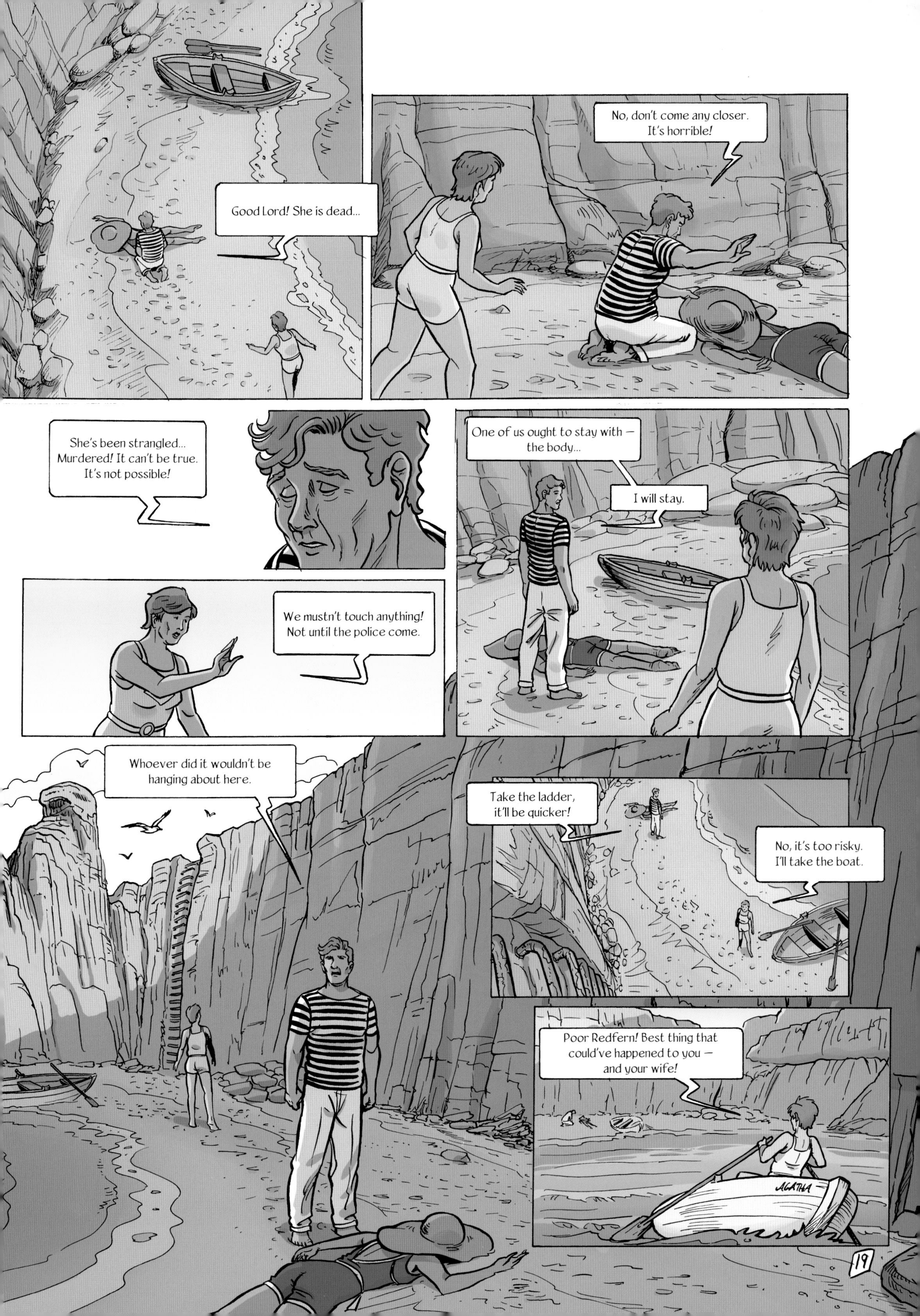
Good Lord! She is dead...
No, don't come any closer. It's horrible!
She's been strangled... Murdered! It can't be true. It's not possible!
We mustn't touch anything! Not until the police come.
One of us ought to stay with — the body...
I will stay.
Whoever did it wouldn't be hanging about here.
Take the ladder, it'll be quicker!
No, it's too risky. I'll take the boat.
Poor Redfern! Best thing that could've happened to you — and your wife!
AGATHA

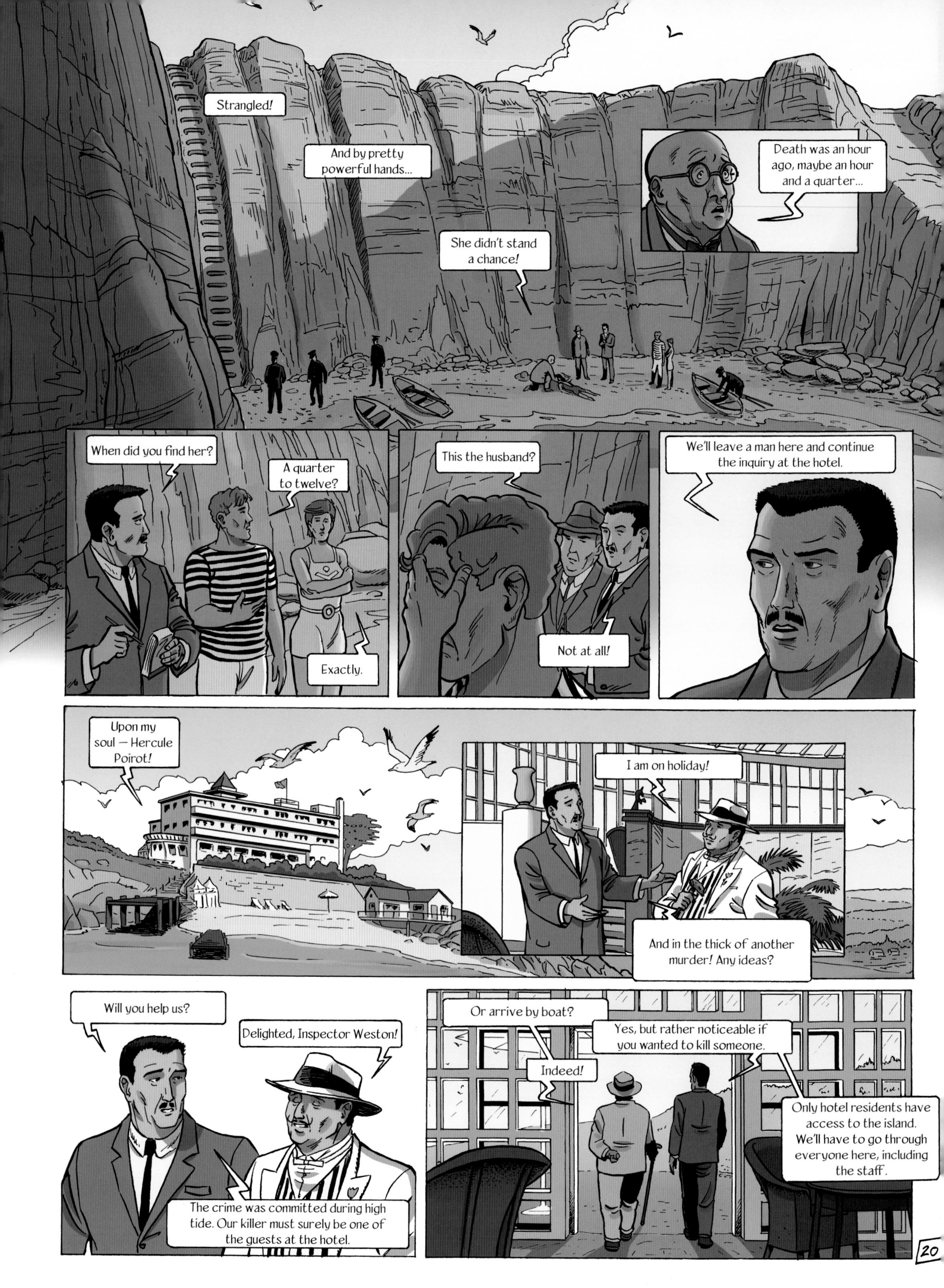

Strangled!
And by pretty powerful hands...
Death was an hour ago, maybe an hour and a quarter...
She didn't stand a chance!
When did you find her?
A quarter to twelve?
Exactly.
This the husband?
Not at all!
We'll leave a man here and continue the inquiry at the hotel.
Upon my soul – Hercule Poirot!
I am on holiday!
And in the thick of another murder! Any ideas?
Will you help us?
Delighted, Inspector Weston!
The crime was committed during high tide. Our killer must surely be one of the guests at the hotel.
Or arrive by boat?
Yes, but rather noticeable if you wanted to kill someone.
Indeed!
Only hotel residents have access to the island. We'll have to go through everyone here, including the staff.
20

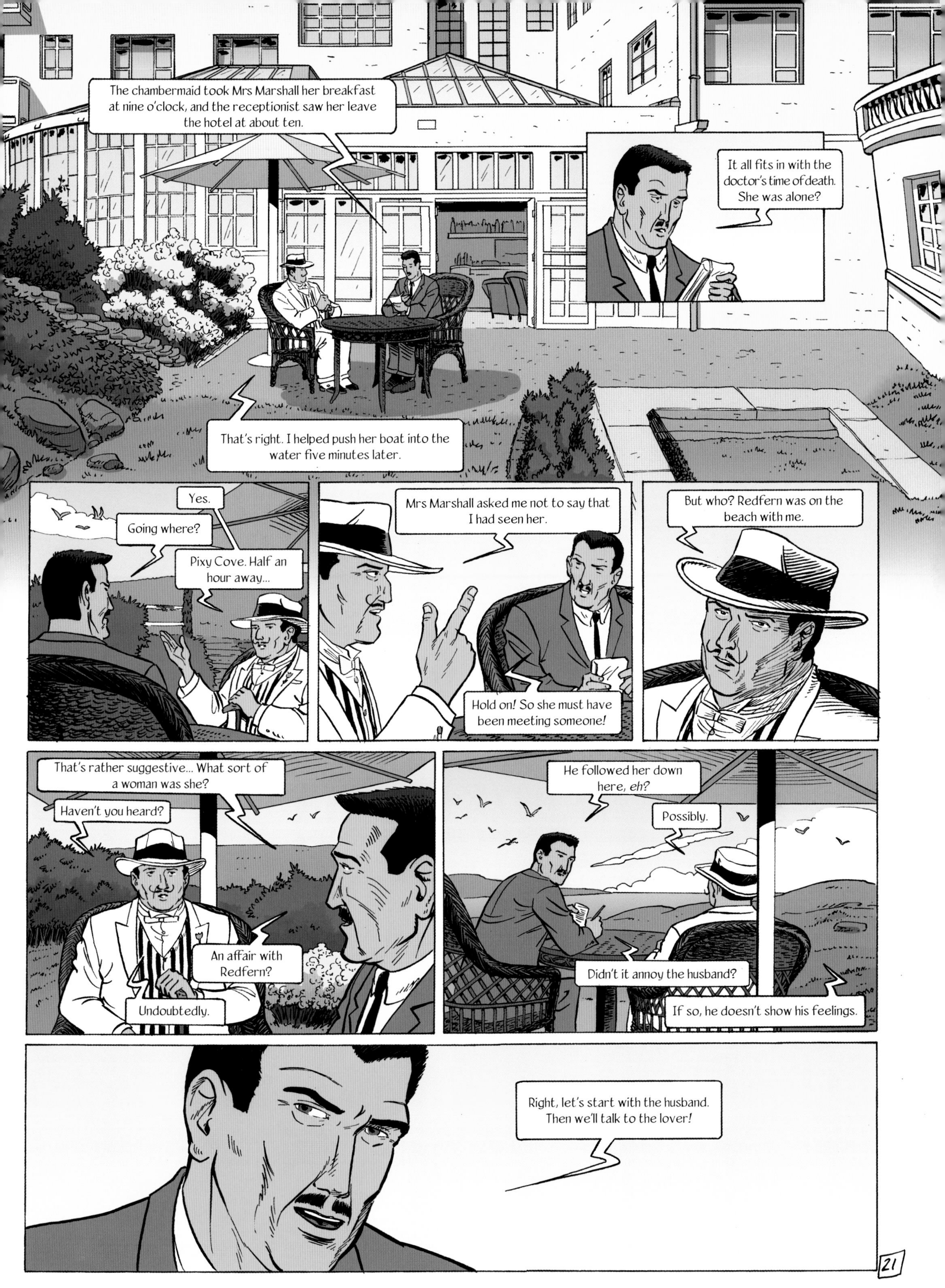
The chambermaid took Mrs Marshall her breakfast at nine o'clock, and the receptionist saw her leave the hotel at about ten.
It all fits in with the doctor's time of death. She was alone?
That's right. I helped push her boat into the water five minutes later.
Going where?
Yes.
Pixy Cove. Half an hour away...
Mrs Marshall asked me not to say that I had seen her.
Hold on! So she must have been meeting someone!
But who? Redfern was on the beach with me.
That's rather suggestive... What sort of a woman was she?
Haven't you heard?
An affair with Redfern?
Undoubtedly.
He followed her down here, *eh?*
Possibly.
Didn't it annoy the husband?
If so, he doesn't show his feelings.
Right, let's start with the husband. Then we'll talk to the lover!
21

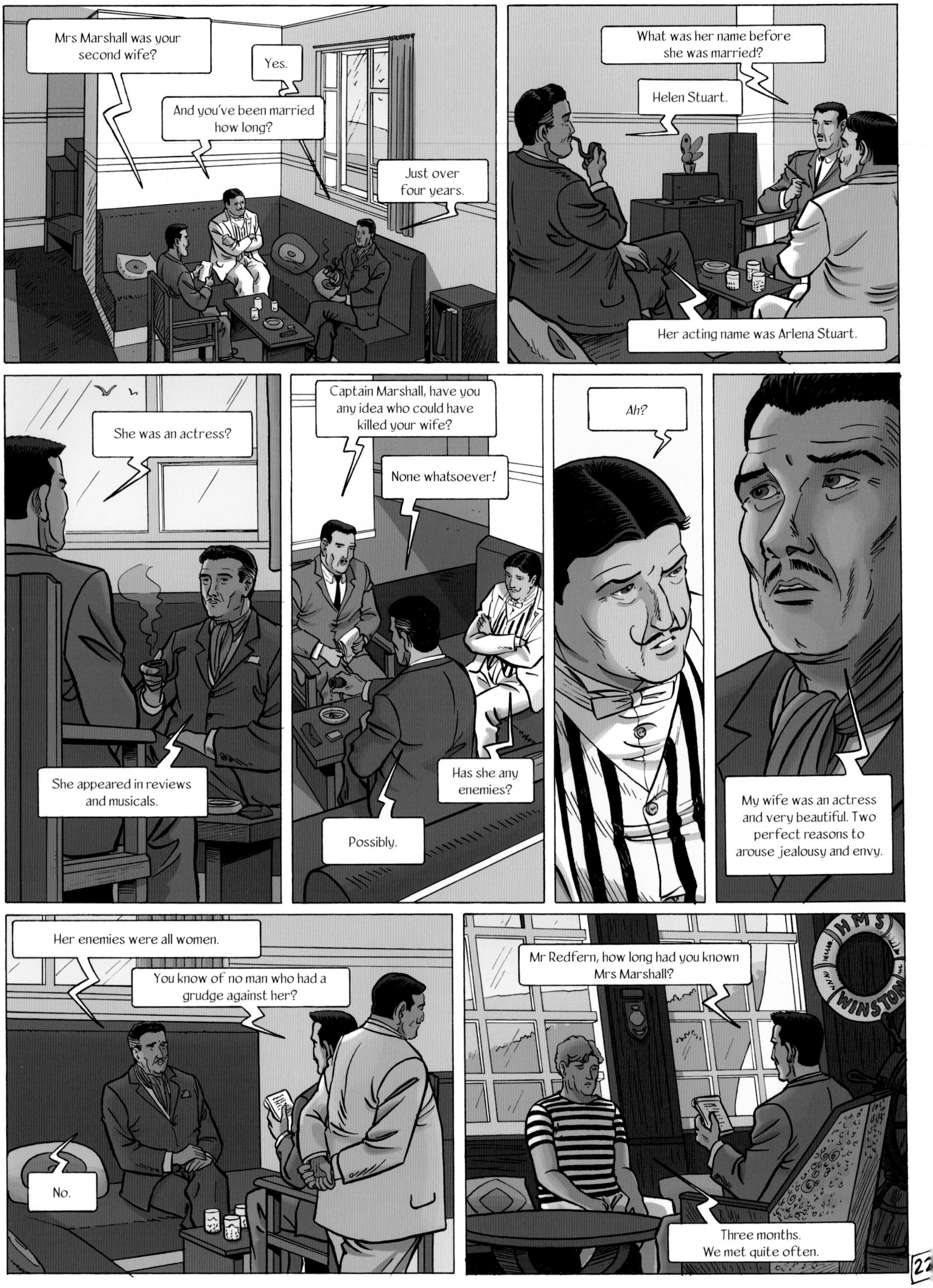
Mrs Marshall was your second wife?
Yes.
And you've been married how long?
Just over four years.
What was her name before she was married?
Helen Stuart.
Her acting name was Arlena Stuart.
She was an actress?
She appeared in reviews and musicals.
Captain Marshall, have you any idea who could have killed your wife?
None whatsoever!
Has she any enemies?
Possibly.
Ah?
My wife was an actress and very beautiful. Two perfect reasons to arouse jealousy and envy.
Her enemies were all women.
You know of no man who had a grudge against her?
No.
Mr Redfern, how long had you known Mrs Marshall?
HMS WINSTON
Three months. We met quite often.
22

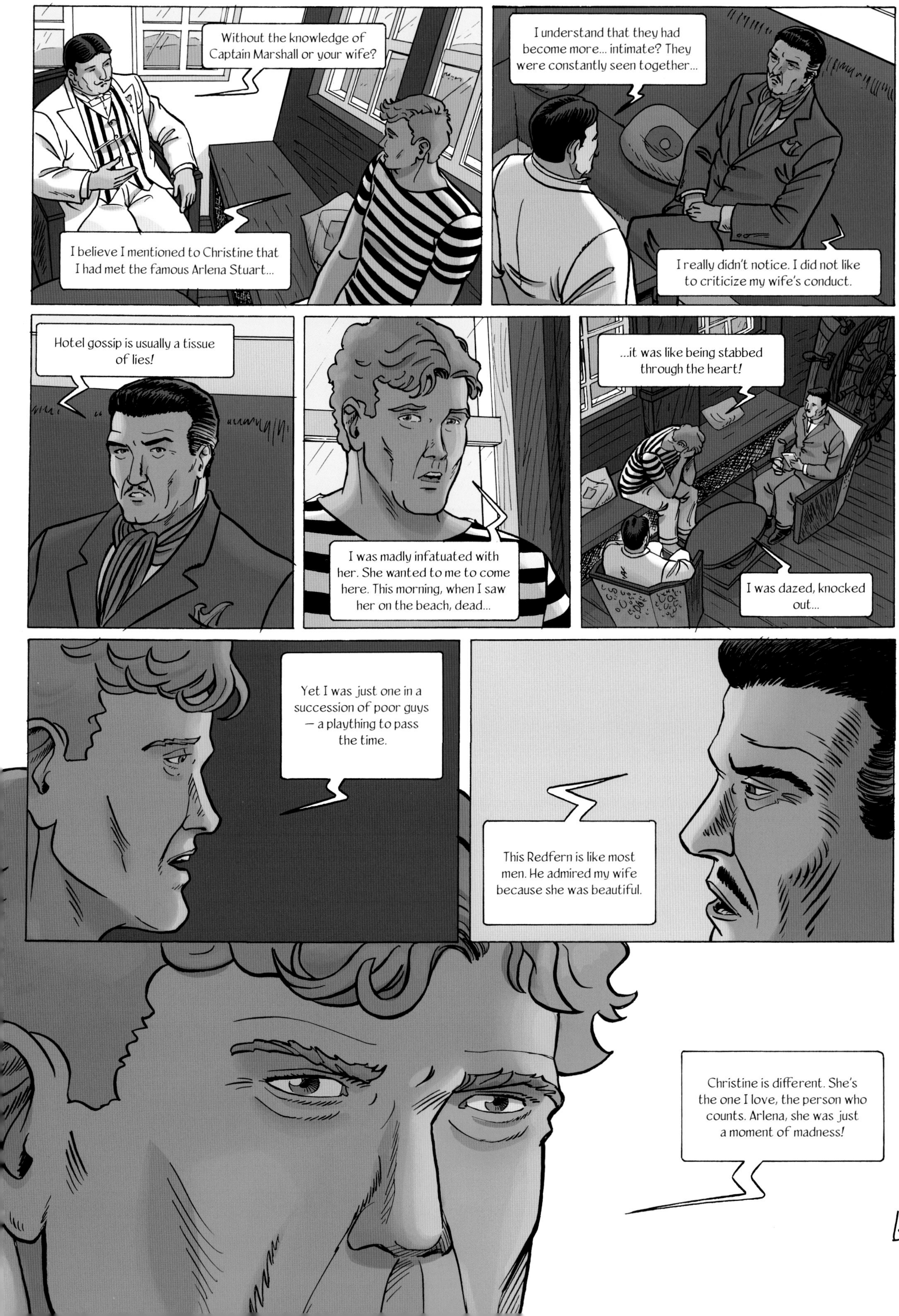
Without the knowledge of Captain Marshall or your wife?
I believe I mentioned to Christine that I had met the famous Arlena Stuart...
I understand that they had become more... intimate? They were constantly seen together...
I really didn't notice. I did not like to criticize my wife's conduct.
Hotel gossip is usually a tissue of lies!
I was madly infatuated with her. She wanted to me to come here. This morning, when I saw her on the beach, dead...
...it was like being stabbed through the heart!
I was dazed, knocked out...
Yet I was just one in a succession of poor guys — a plaything to pass the time.
This Redfern is like most men. He admired my wife because she was beautiful.
Christine is different. She's the one I love, the person who counts. Arlena, she was just a moment of madness!

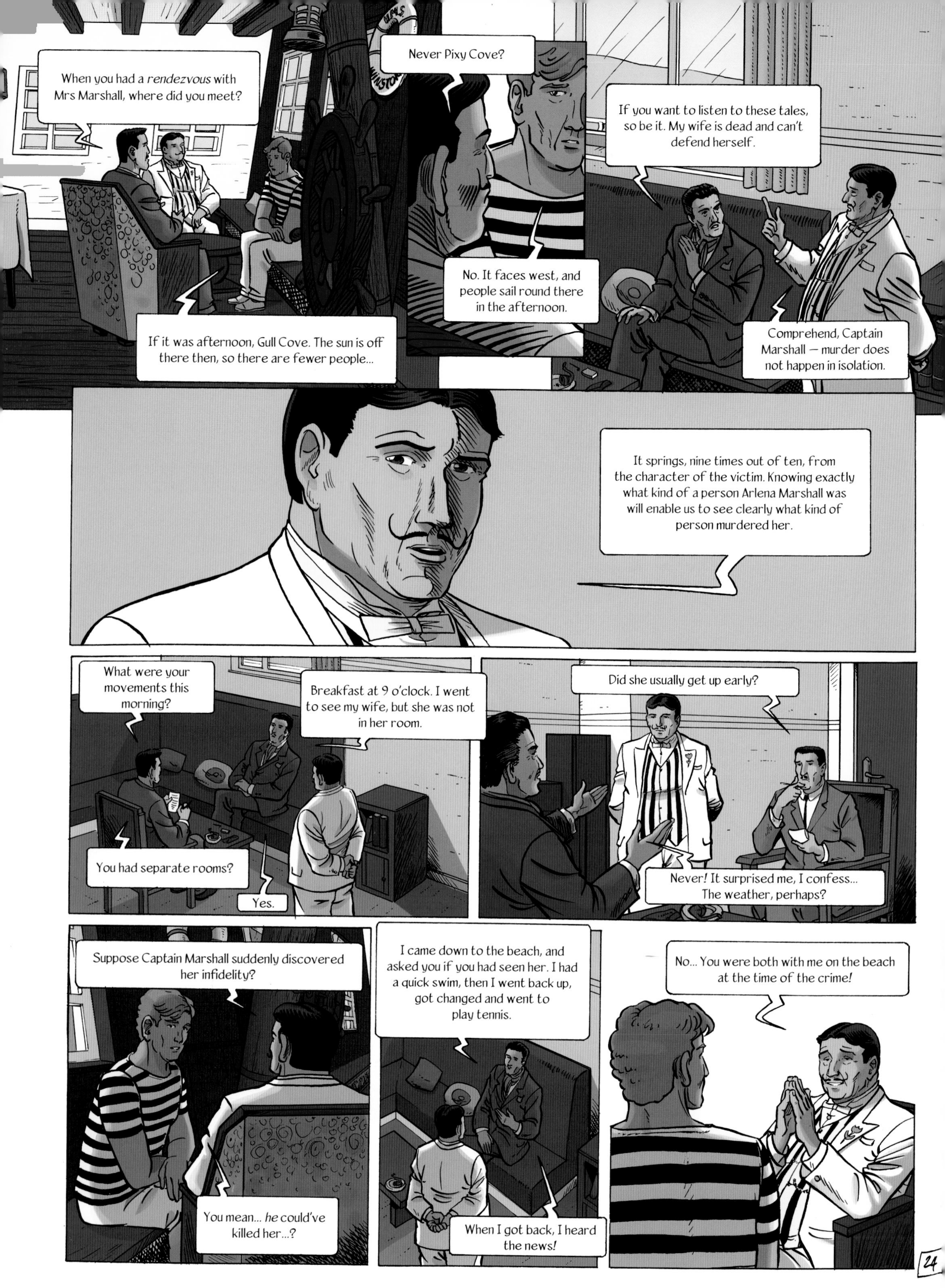
When you had a *rendezvous* with Mrs Marshall, where did you meet?
If it was afternoon, Gull Cove. The sun is off there then, so there are fewer people...
Never Pixy Cove?
No. It faces west, and people sail round there in the afternoon.
If you want to listen to these tales, so be it. My wife is dead and can't defend herself.
Comprehend, Captain Marshall — murder does not happen in isolation.
It springs, nine times out of ten, from the character of the victim. Knowing exactly what kind of a person Arlena Marshall was will enable us to see clearly what kind of person murdered her.
What were your movements this morning?
Breakfast at 9 o'clock. I went to see my wife, but she was not in her room.
You had separate rooms?
Yes.
Did she usually get up early?
Never! It surprised me, I confess... The weather, perhaps?
Suppose Captain Marshall suddenly discovered her infidelity?
You mean... *he* could've killed her...?
I came down to the beach, and asked you if you had seen her. I had a quick swim, then I went back up, got changed and went to play tennis.
When I got back, I heard the news!
No... You were both with me on the beach at the time of the crime!
24

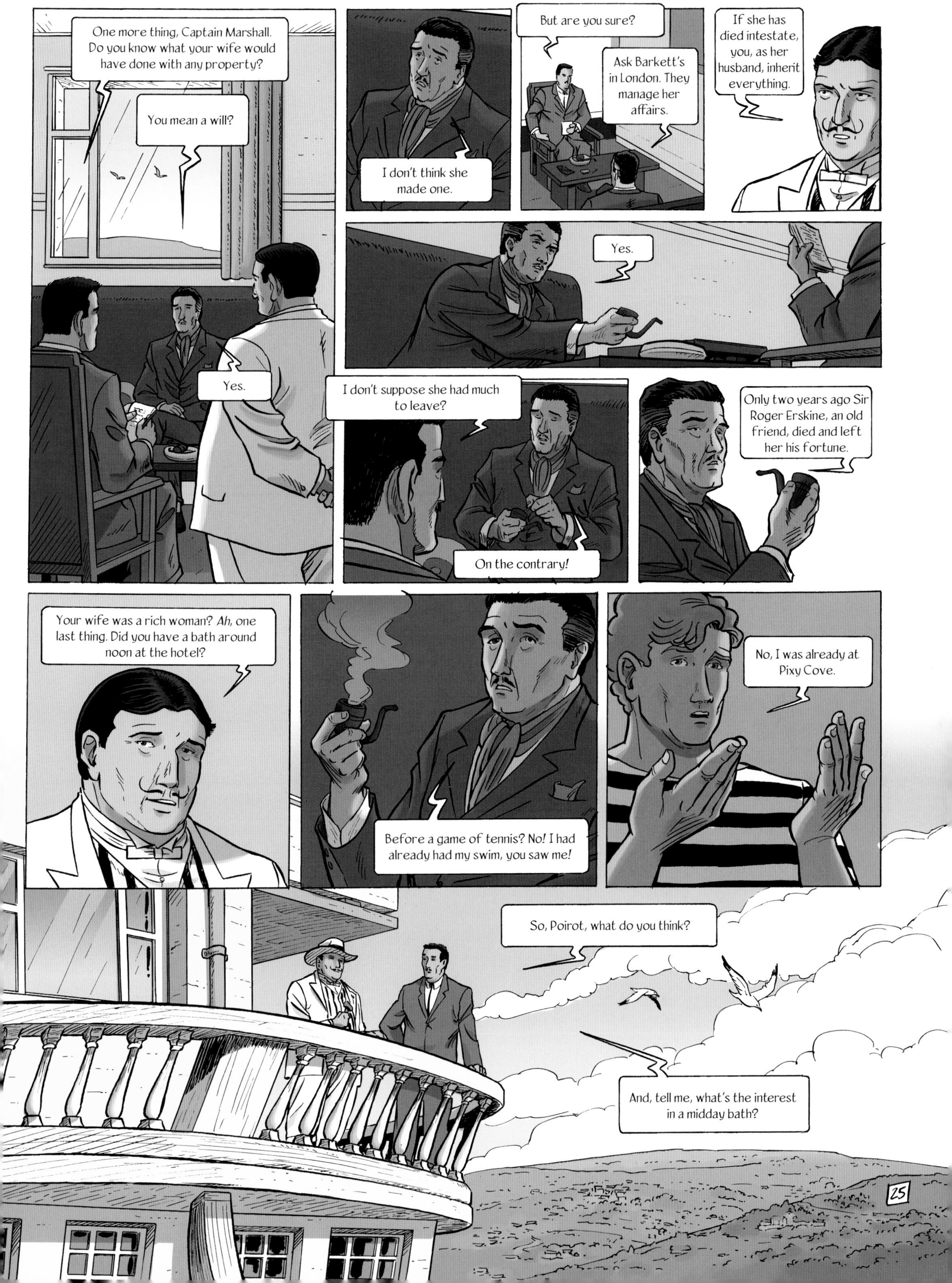

One more thing, Captain Marshall. Do you know what your wife would have done with any property?
You mean a will?
I don't think she made one.
But are you sure?
Ask Barkett's in London. They manage her affairs.
If she has died intestate, you, as her husband, inherit everything.
Yes.
Yes.
I don't suppose she had much to leave?
On the contrary!
Only two years ago Sir Roger Erskine, an old friend, died and left her his fortune.
Your wife was a rich woman? *Ah*, one last thing. Did you have a bath around noon at the hotel?
Before a game of tennis? No! I had already had my swim, you saw me!
No, I was already at Pixy Cove.
So, Poirot, what do you think?
And, tell me, what's the interest in a midday bath?

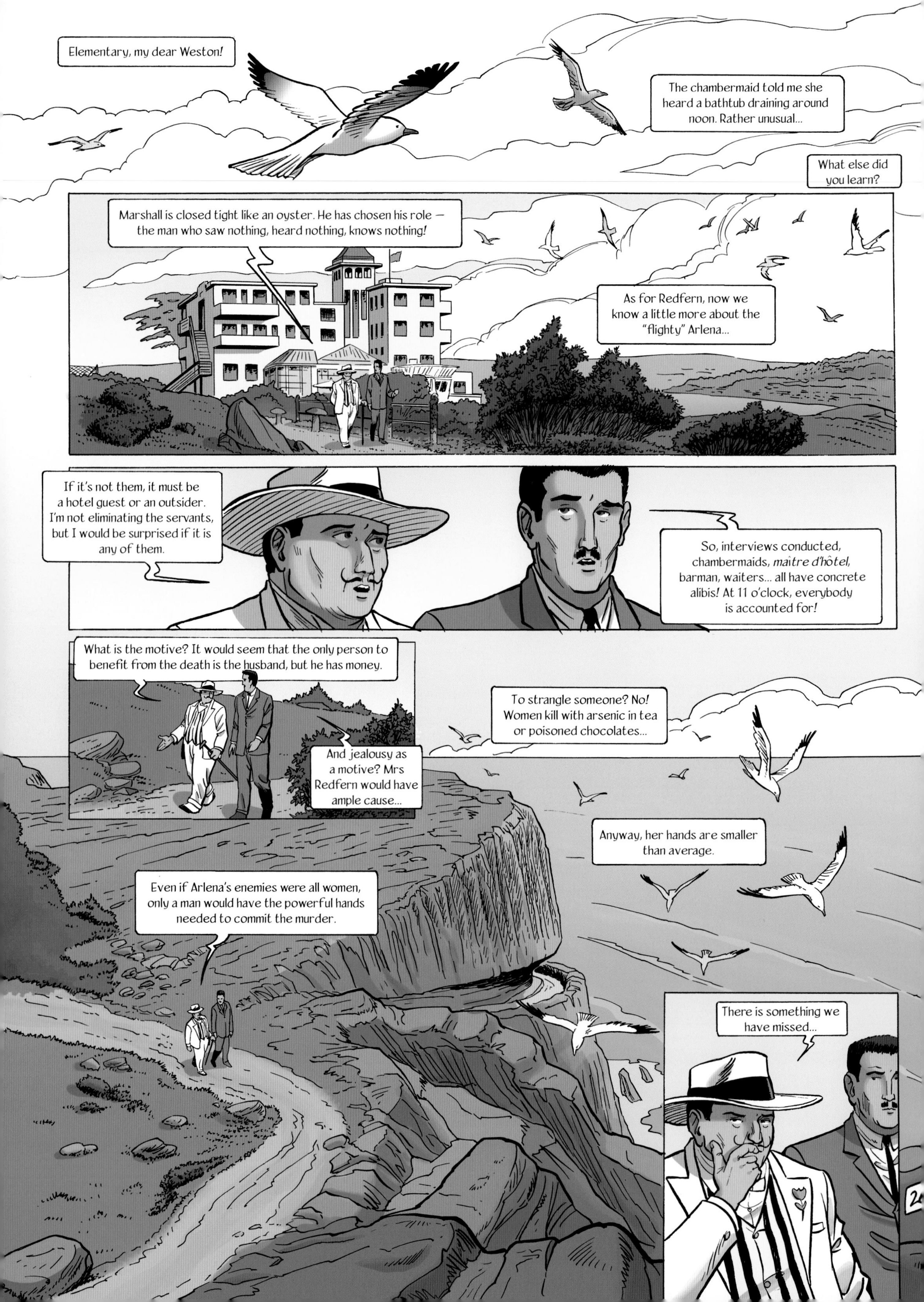
Elementary, my dear Weston!
The chambermaid told me she heard a bathtub draining around noon. Rather unusual...
What else did you learn?
Marshall is closed tight like an oyster. He has chosen his role — the man who saw nothing, heard nothing, knows nothing!
As for Redfern, now we know a little more about the "flighty" Arlena...
If it's not them, it must be a hotel guest or an outsider. I'm not eliminating the servants, but I would be surprised if it is any of them.
So, interviews conducted, chambermaids, *maître d'hôtel*, barman, waiters... all have concrete alibis! At 11 o'clock, everybody is accounted for!
What is the motive? It would seem that the only person to benefit from the death is the husband, but he has money.
And jealousy as a motive? Mrs Redfern would have ample cause...
To strangle someone? No! Women kill with arsenic in tea or poisoned chocolates...
Anyway, her hands are smaller than average.
Even if Arlena's enemies were all women, only a man would have the powerful hands needed to commit the murder.
There is something we have missed...

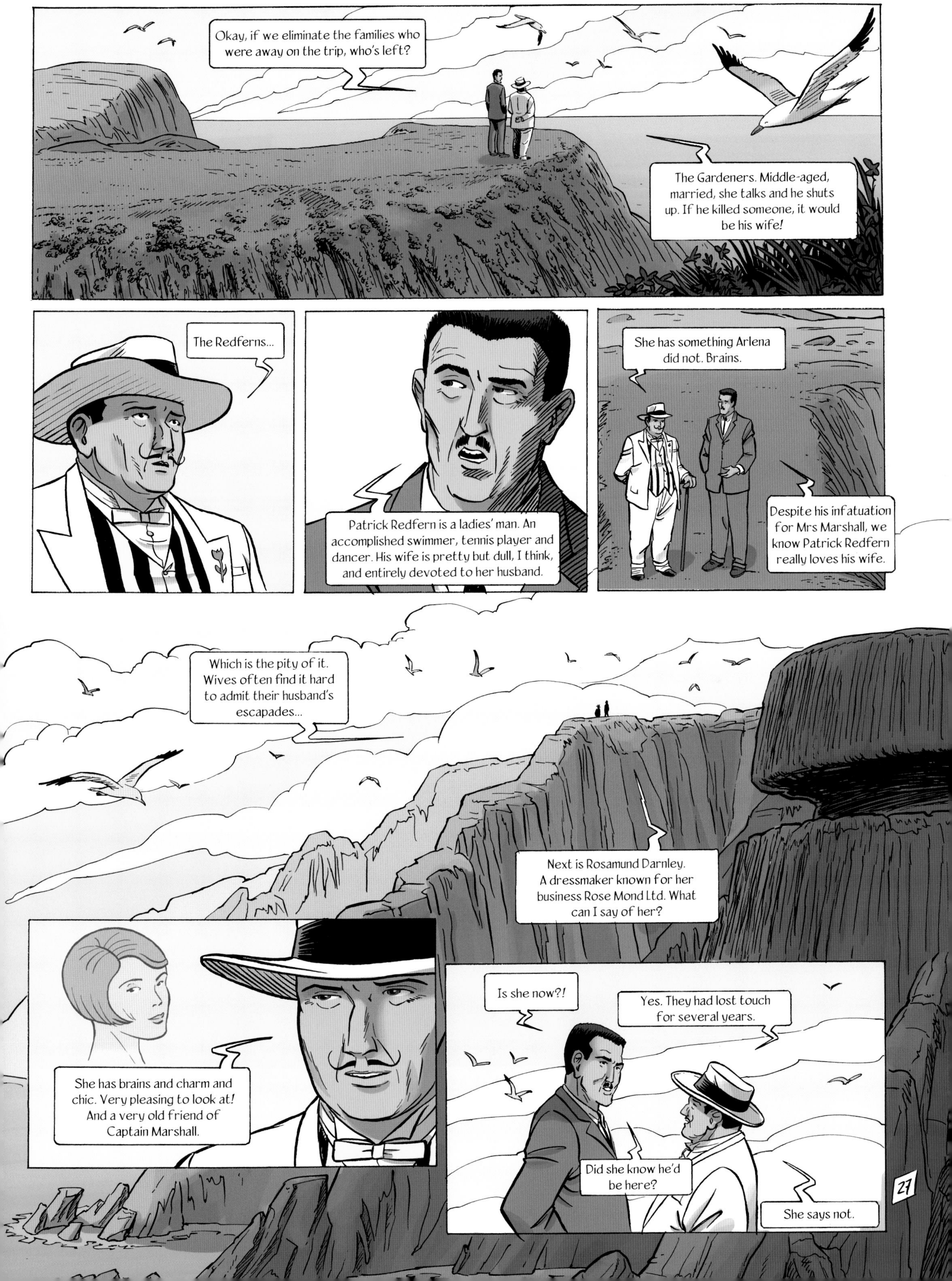
Okay, if we eliminate the families who were away on the trip, who's left?
The Gardeners. Middle-aged, married, she talks and he shuts up. If he killed someone, it would be his wife!
The Redferns...
Patrick Redfern is a ladies' man. An accomplished swimmer, tennis player and dancer. His wife is pretty but dull, I think, and entirely devoted to her husband.
She has something Arlena did not. Brains.
Despite his infatuation for Mrs Marshall, we know Patrick Redfern really loves his wife.
Which is the pity of it. Wives often find it hard to admit their husband's escapades...
Next is Rosamund Darnley. A dressmaker known for her business Rose Mond Ltd. What can I say of her?
She has brains and charm and chic. Very pleasing to look at! And a very old friend of Captain Marshall.
Is she now?!
Yes. They had lost touch for several years.
Did she know he'd be here?
She says not.

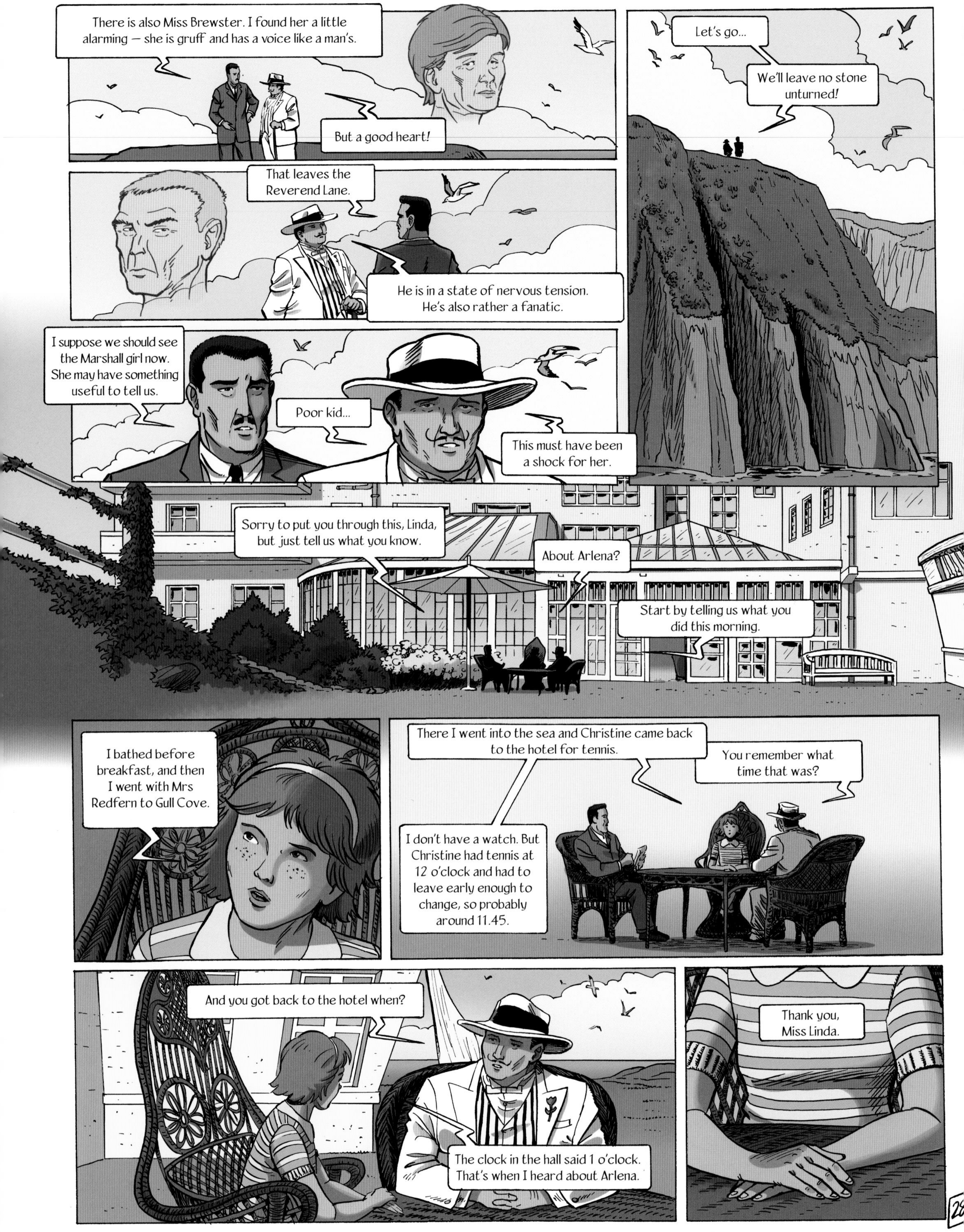
There is also Miss Brewster. I found her a little alarming — she is gruff and has a voice like a man's.
But a good heart!
That leaves the Reverend Lane.
He is in a state of nervous tension. He's also rather a fanatic.
I suppose we should see the Marshall girl now. She may have something useful to tell us.
Poor kid...
This must have been a shock for her.
Let's go...
We'll leave no stone unturned!
Sorry to put you through this, Linda, but just tell us what you know.
About Arlena?
Start by telling us what you did this morning.
I bathed before breakfast, and then I went with Mrs Redfern to Gull Cove.
There I went into the sea and Christine came back to the hotel for tennis.
You remember what time that was?
I don't have a watch. But Christine had tennis at 12 o'clock and had to leave early enough to change, so probably around 11.45.
And you got back to the hotel when?
The clock in the hall said 1 o'clock. That's when I heard about Arlena.
Thank you, Miss Linda.
28

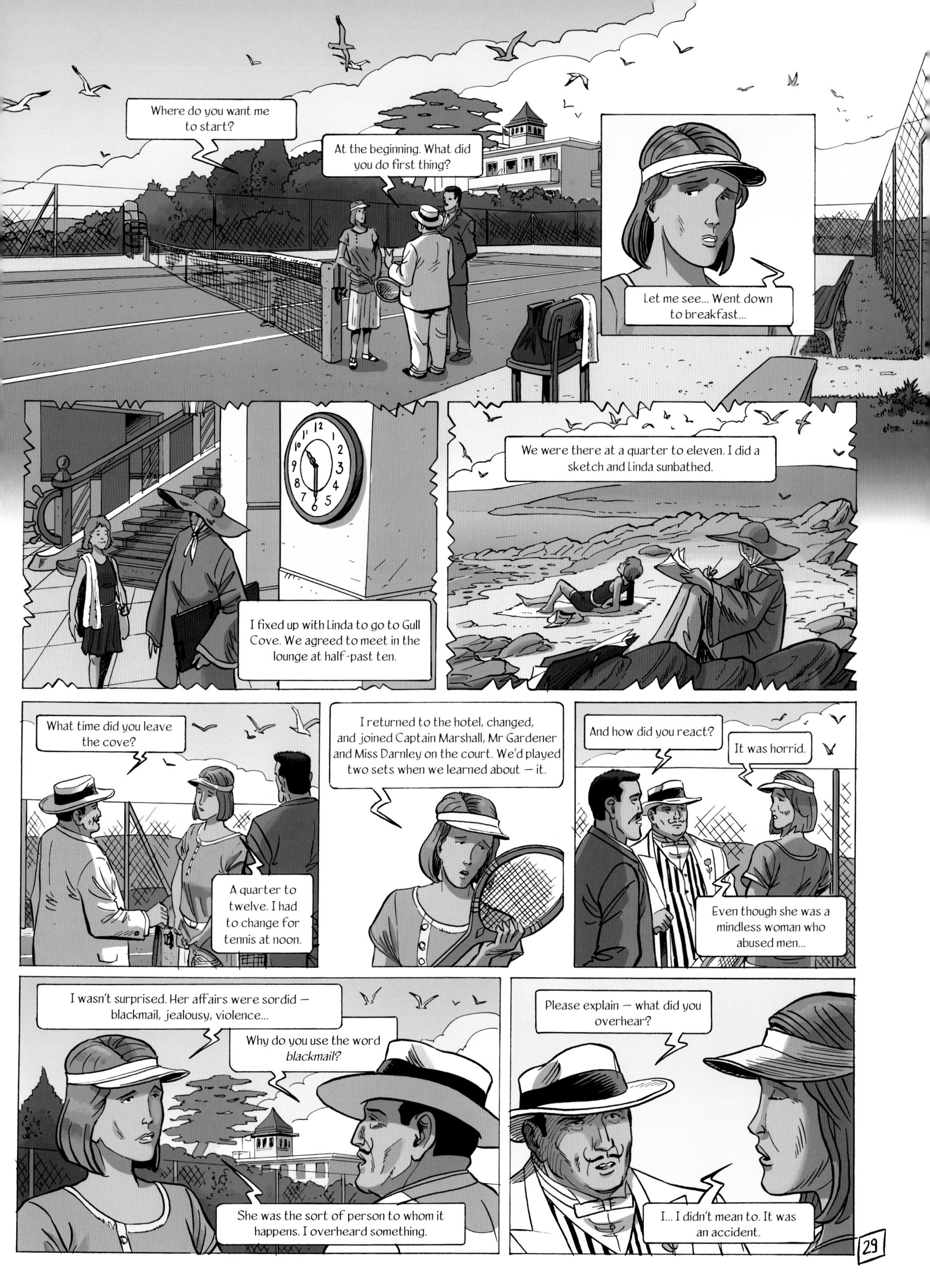
Where do you want me to start?
At the beginning. What did you do first thing?
Let me see... Went down to breakfast...
I fixed up with Linda to go to Gull Cove. We agreed to meet in the lounge at half-past ten.
We were there at a quarter to eleven. I did a sketch and Linda sunbathed.
What time did you leave the cove?
A quarter to twelve. I had to change for tennis at noon.
I returned to the hotel, changed, and joined Captain Marshall, Mr Gardener and Miss Darnley on the court. We'd played two sets when we learned about – it.
And how did you react?
It was horrid.
Even though she was a mindless woman who abused men...
I wasn't surprised. Her affairs were sordid – blackmail, jealousy, violence...
Why do you use the word *blackmail*?
She was the sort of person to whom it happens. I overheard something.
Please explain – what did you overhear?
I... I didn't mean to. It was an accident.
29

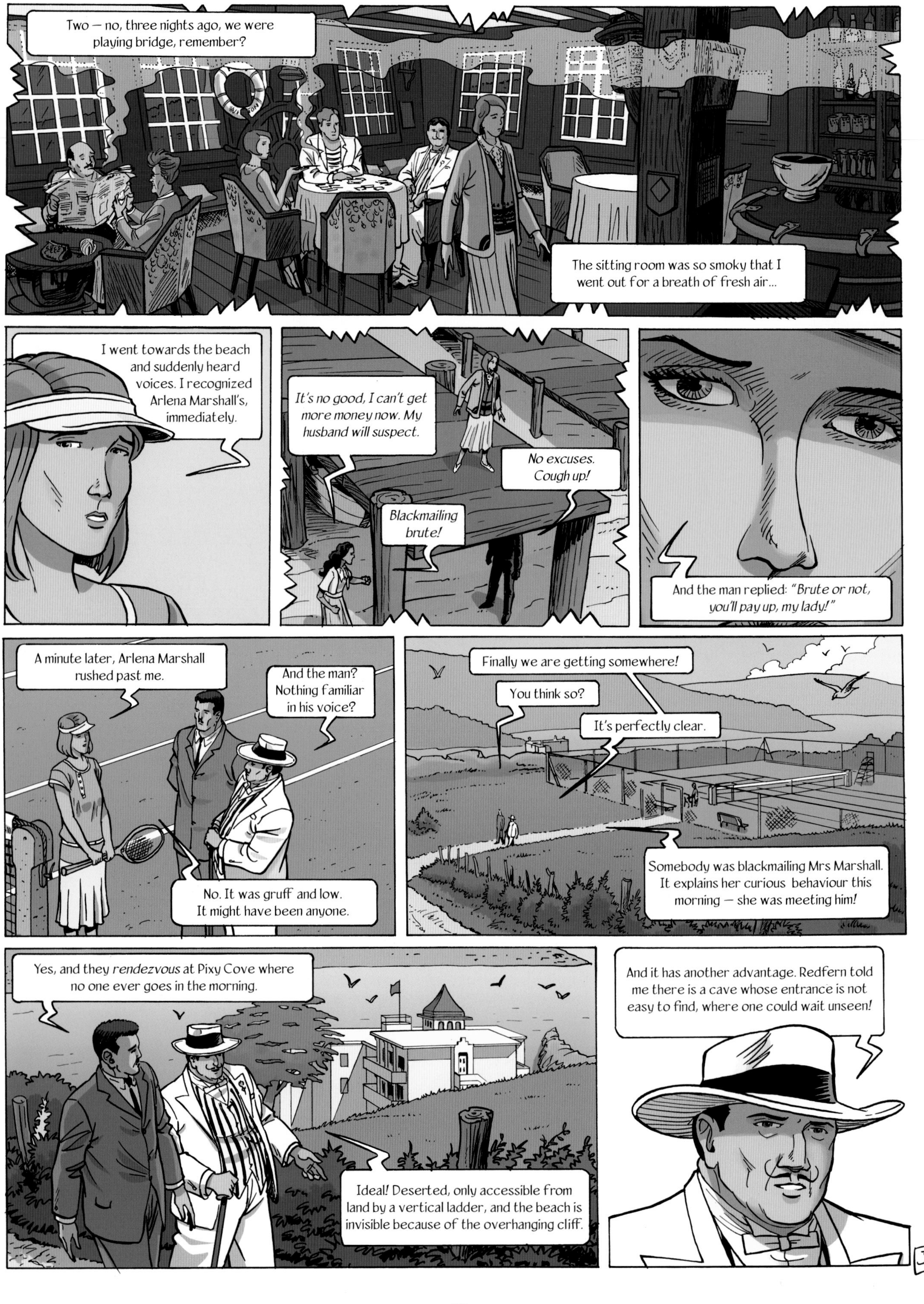
Two — no, three nights ago, we were playing bridge, remember?
The sitting room was so smoky that I went out for a breath of fresh air...
I went towards the beach and suddenly heard voices. I recognized Arlena Marshall's, immediately.
It's no good, I can't get more money now. My husband will suspect.
No excuses. Cough up!
Blackmailing brute!
And the man replied: *"Brute or not, you'll pay up, my lady!"*
A minute later, Arlena Marshall rushed past me.
And the man? Nothing familiar in his voice?
No. It was gruff and low. It might have been anyone.
Finally we are getting somewhere!
You think so?
It's perfectly clear.
Somebody was blackmailing Mrs Marshall. It explains her curious behaviour this morning — she was meeting him!
Yes, and they *rendezvous* at Pixy Cove where no one ever goes in the morning.
Ideal! Deserted, only accessible from land by a vertical ladder, and the beach is invisible because of the overhanging cliff.
And it has another advantage. Redfern told me there is a cave whose entrance is not easy to find, where one could wait unseen!

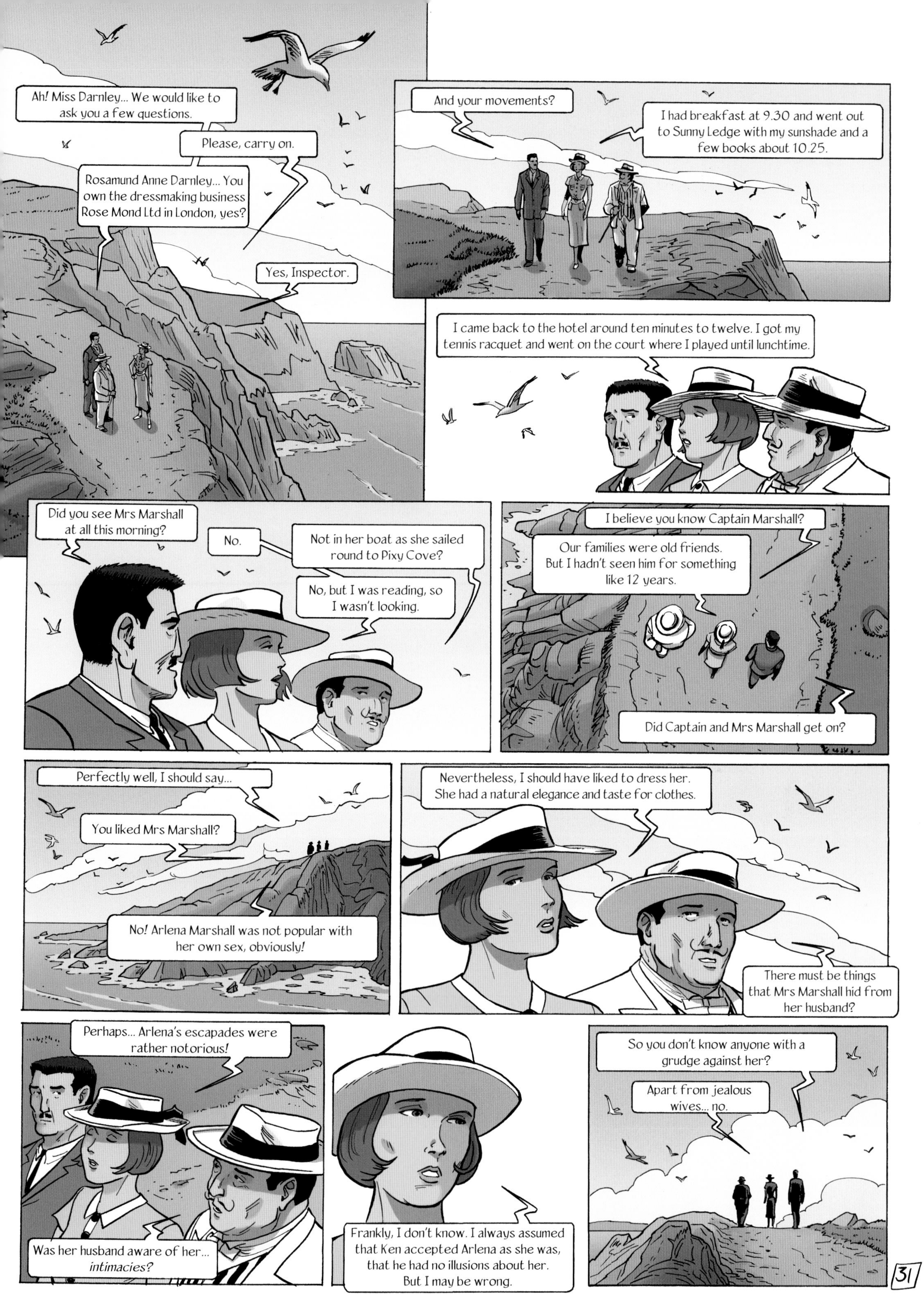
Ah! Miss Darnley... We would like to ask you a few questions.
Please, carry on.
Rosamund Anne Darnley... You own the dressmaking business Rose Mond Ltd in London, yes?
Yes, Inspector.
And your movements?
I had breakfast at 9.30 and went out to Sunny Ledge with my sunshade and a few books about 10.25.
I came back to the hotel around ten minutes to twelve. I got my tennis racquet and went on the court where I played until lunchtime.
Did you see Mrs Marshall at all this morning?
No.
Not in her boat as she sailed round to Pixy Cove?
No, but I was reading, so I wasn't looking.
I believe you know Captain Marshall?
Our families were old friends. But I hadn't seen him for something like 12 years.
Did Captain and Mrs Marshall get on?
Perfectly well, I should say...
You liked Mrs Marshall?
No! Arlena Marshall was not popular with her own sex, obviously!
Nevertheless, I should have liked to dress her. She had a natural elegance and taste for clothes.
There must be things that Mrs Marshall hid from her husband?
Perhaps... Arlena's escapades were rather notorious!
Was her husband aware of her... intimacies?
Frankly, I don't know. I always assumed that Ken accepted Arlena as she was, that he had no illusions about her. But I may be wrong.
So you don't know anyone with a grudge against her?
Apart from jealous wives... no.
31

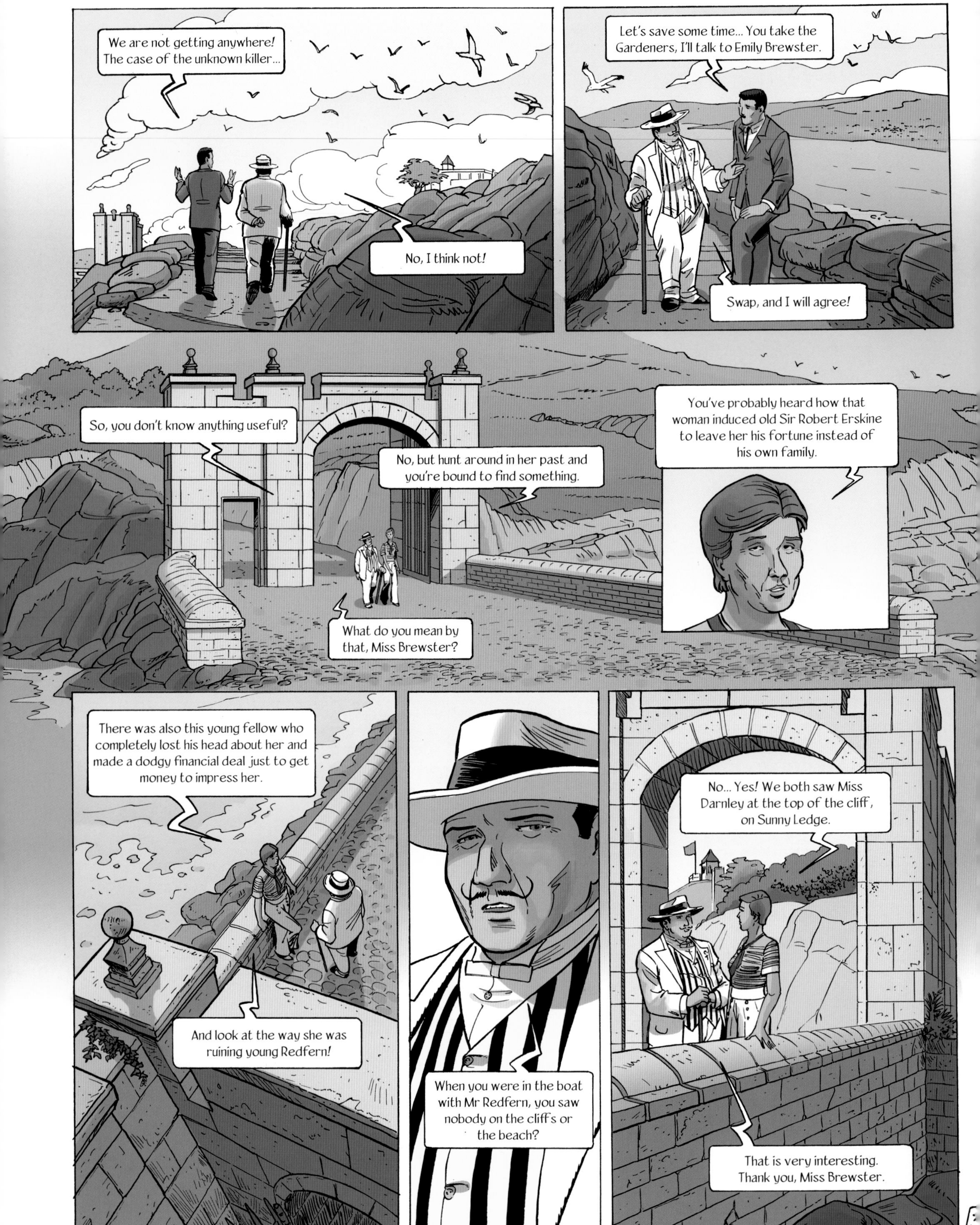
We are not getting anywhere! The case of the unknown killer...
No, I think not!
Let's save some time... You take the Gardeners, I'll talk to Emily Brewster.
Swap, and I will agree!
So, you don't know anything useful?
No, but hunt around in her past and you're bound to find something.
What do you mean by that, Miss Brewster?
You've probably heard how that woman induced old Sir Robert Erskine to leave her his fortune instead of his own family.
There was also this young fellow who completely lost his head about her and made a dodgy financial deal just to get money to impress her.
And look at the way she was ruining young Redfern!
When you were in the boat with Mr Redfern, you saw nobody on the cliffs or the beach?
No... Yes! We both saw Miss Darnley at the top of the cliff, on Sunny Ledge.
That is very interesting. Thank you, Miss Brewster.

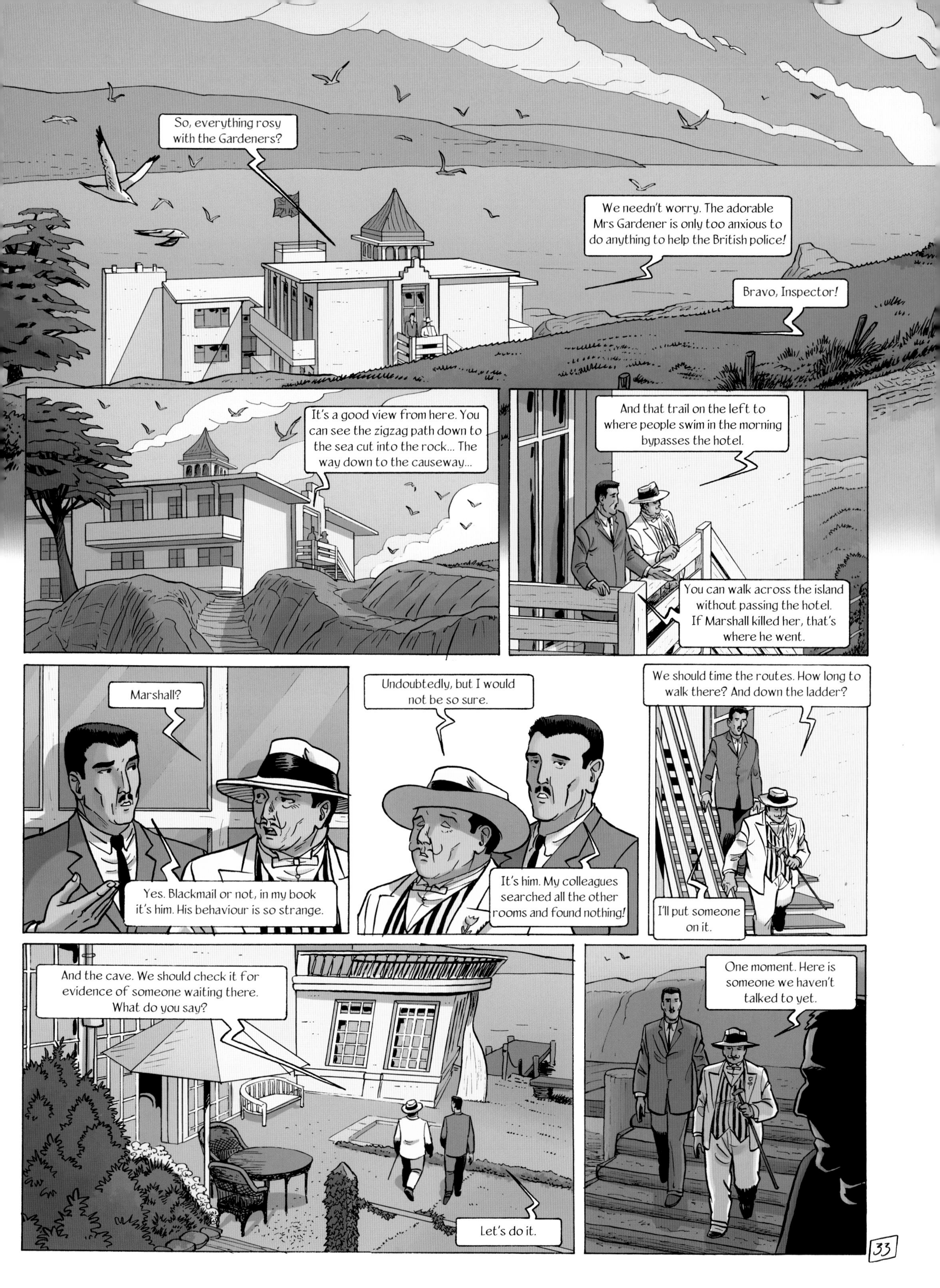
So, everything rosy with the Gardeners?
We needn't worry. The adorable Mrs Gardener is only too anxious to do anything to help the British police!
Bravo, Inspector!
It's a good view from here. You can see the zigzag path down to the sea cut into the rock... The way down to the causeway...
And that trail on the left to where people swim in the morning bypasses the hotel.
You can walk across the island without passing the hotel. If Marshall killed her, that's where he went.
Marshall?
Yes. Blackmail or not, in my book it's him. His behaviour is so strange.
Undoubtedly, but I would not be so sure.
It's him. My colleagues searched all the other rooms and found nothing!
We should time the routes. How long to walk there? And down the ladder?
I'll put someone on it.
And the cave. We should check it for evidence of someone waiting there. What do you say?
Let's do it.
One moment. Here is someone we haven't talked to yet.
33

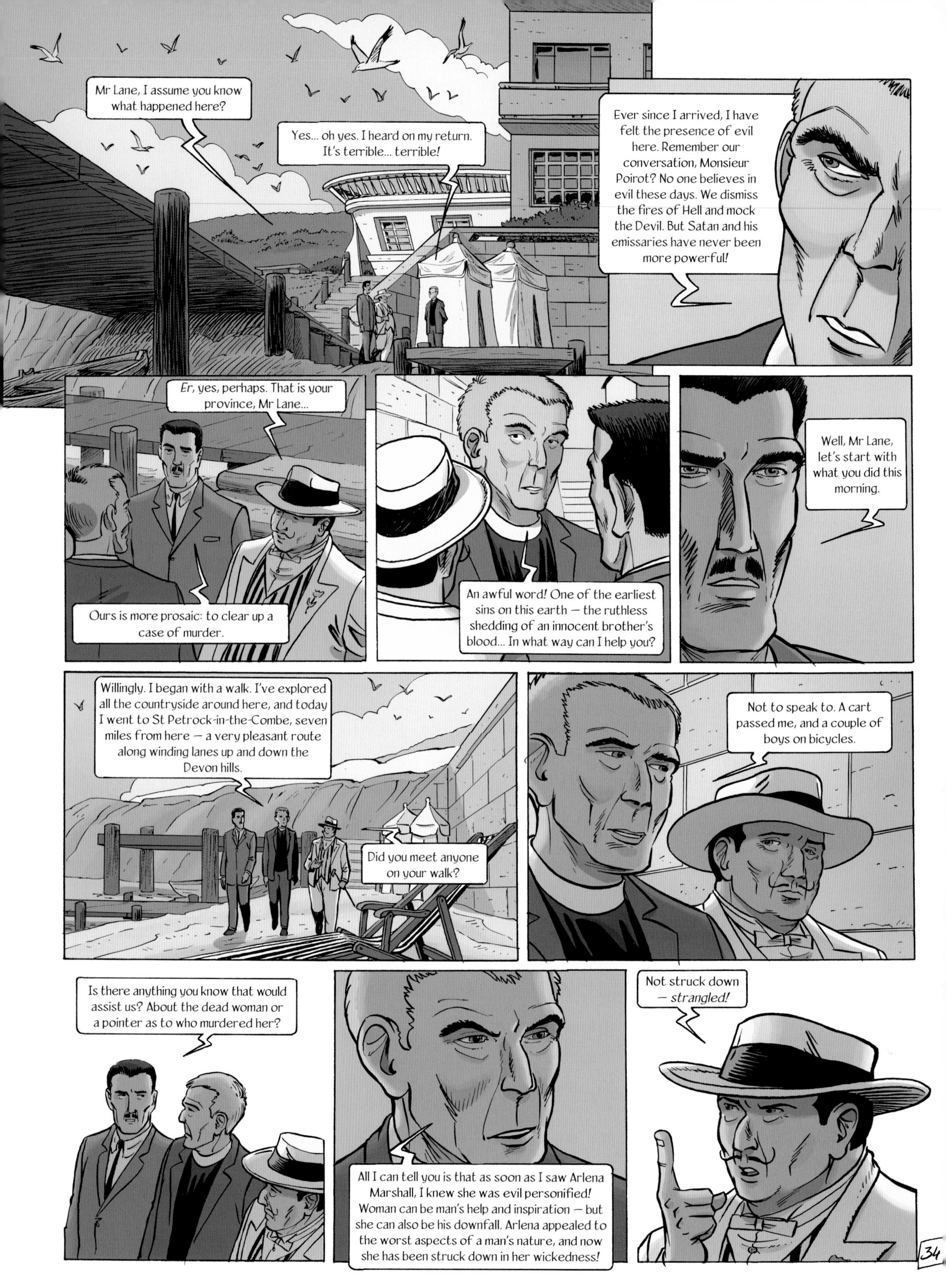
Mr Lane, I assume you know what happened here?
Yes... oh yes. I heard on my return. It's terrible... terrible!
Ever since I arrived, I have felt the presence of evil here. Remember our conversation, Monsieur Poirot? No one believes in evil these days. We dismiss the fires of Hell and mock the Devil. But Satan and his emissaries have never been more powerful!
Er, yes, perhaps. That is your province, Mr Lane...
Ours is more prosaic: to clear up a case of murder.
An awful word! One of the earliest sins on this earth — the ruthless shedding of an innocent brother's blood... In what way can I help you?
Well, Mr Lane, let's start with what you did this morning.
Willingly. I began with a walk. I've explored all the countryside around here, and today I went to St Petrock-in-the-Combe, seven miles from here — a very pleasant route along winding lanes up and down the Devon hills.
Did you meet anyone on your walk?
Not to speak to. A cart passed me, and a couple of boys on bicycles.
Is there anything you know that would assist us? About the dead woman or a pointer as to who murdered her?
All I can tell you is that as soon as I saw Arlena Marshall, I knew she was evil personified! Woman can be man's help and inspiration — but she can also be his downfall. Arlena appealed to the worst aspects of a man's nature, and now she has been struck down in her wickedness!
Not struck down — *strangled!*
34

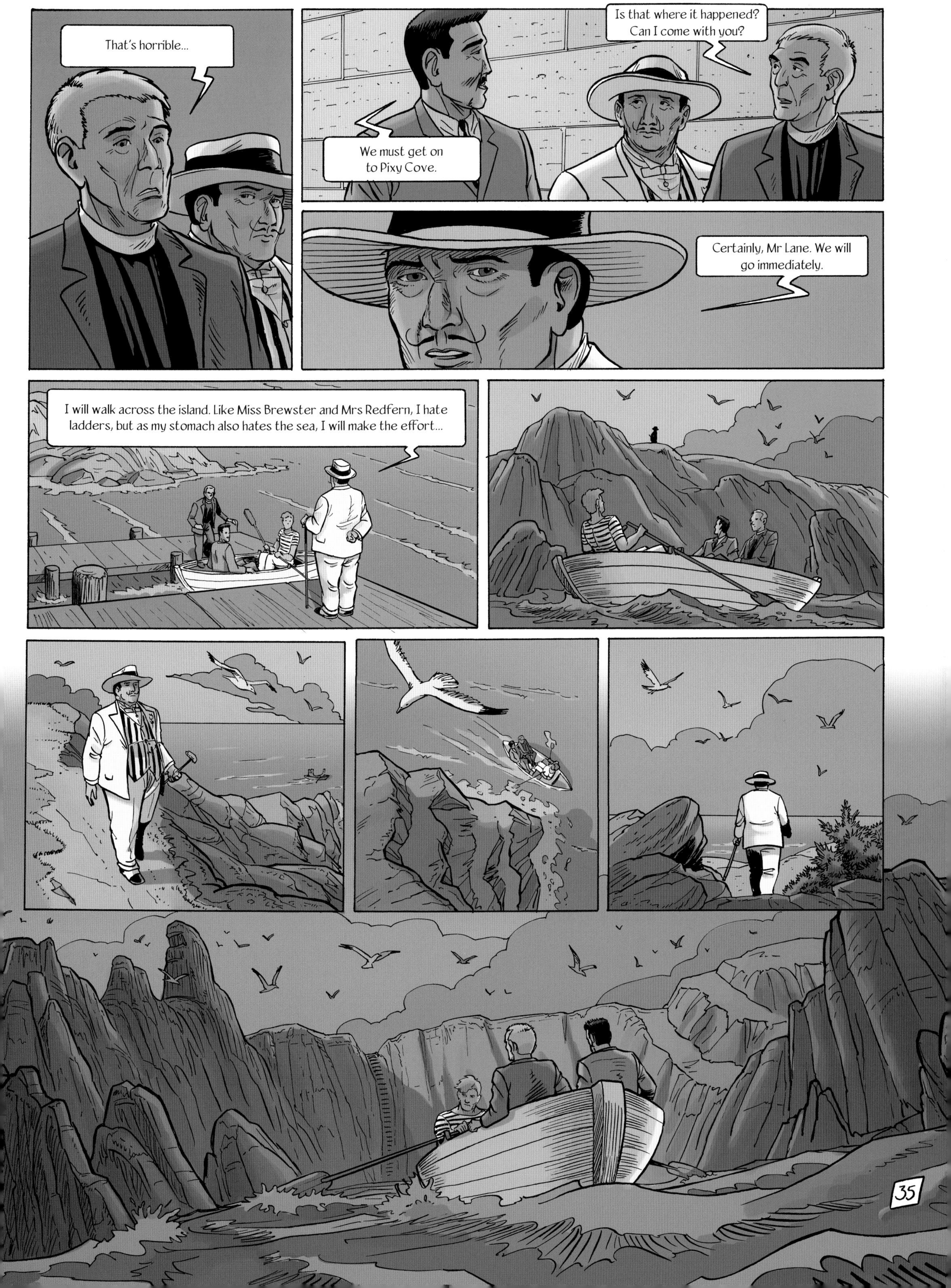
That's horrible...
Is that where it happened? Can I come with you?
We must get on to Pixy Cove.
Certainly, Mr Lane. We will go immediately.
I will walk across the island. Like Miss Brewster and Mrs Redfern, I hate ladders, but as my stomach also hates the sea, I will make the effort...

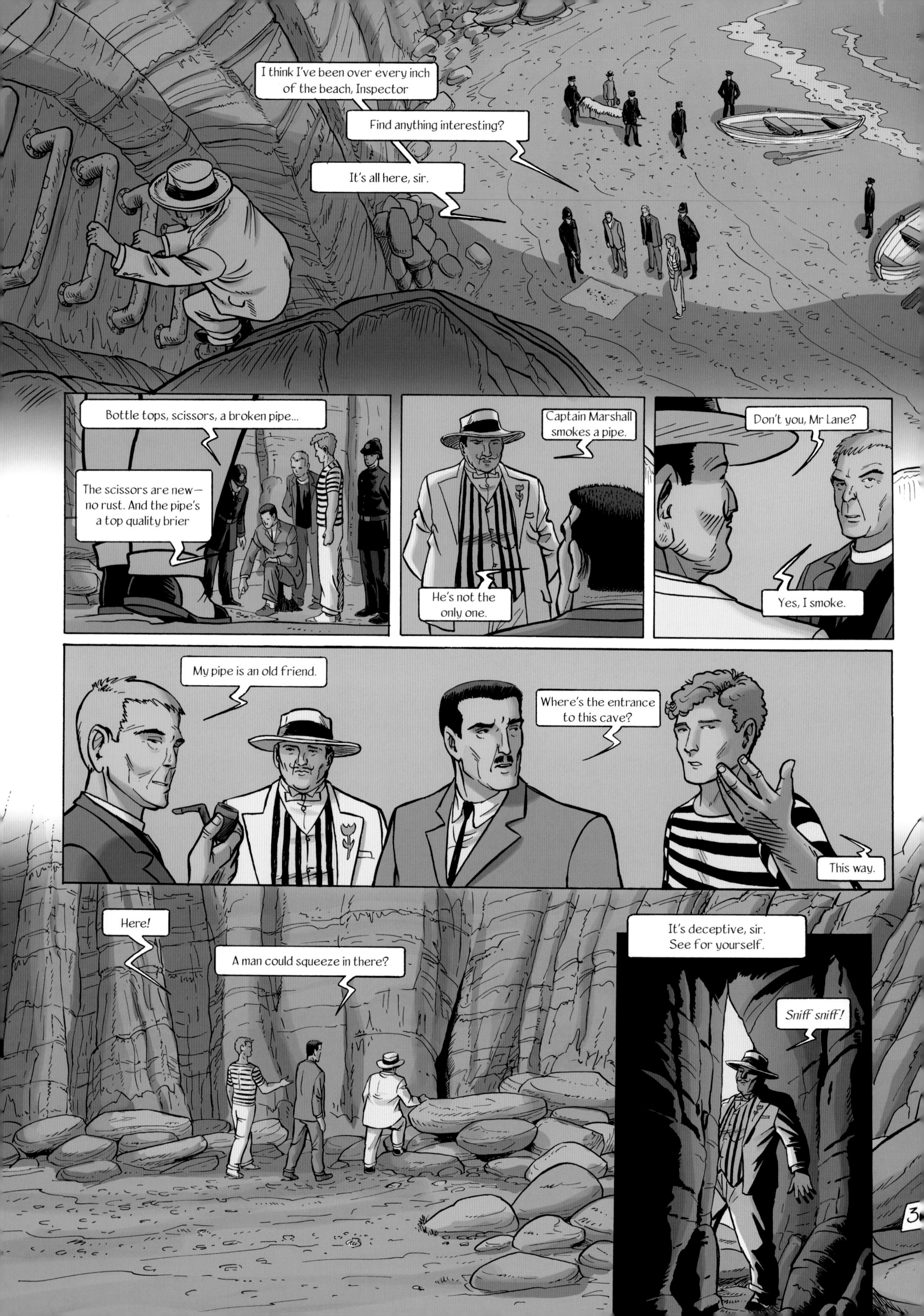

I think I've been over every inch of the beach, Inspector
Find anything interesting?
It's all here, sir.
Bottle tops, scissors, a broken pipe...
The scissors are new—no rust. And the pipe's a top quality brier
Captain Marshall smokes a pipe.
He's not the only one.
Don't you, Mr Lane?
Yes, I smoke.
My pipe is an old friend.
Where's the entrance to this cave?
This way.
Here!
A man could squeeze in there?
It's deceptive, sir. See for yourself.
Sniff sniff!

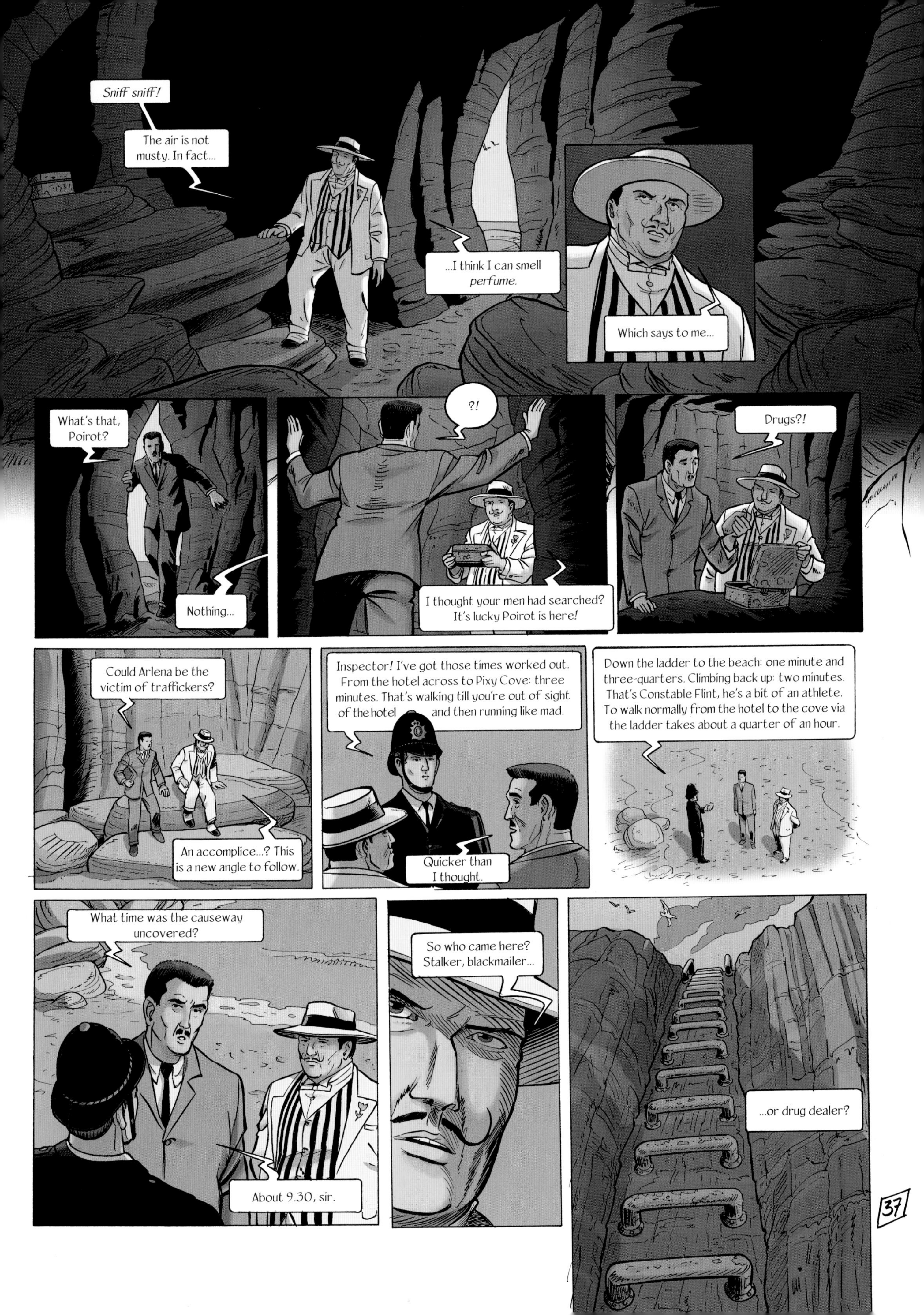

Sniff sniff!
The air is not musty. In fact...
...I think I can smell *perfume.*
Which says to me...
What's that, Poirot?
Nothing...
?!
I thought your men had searched? It's lucky Poirot is here!
Drugs?!
Could Arlena be the victim of traffickers?
An accomplice...? This is a new angle to follow.
Inspector! I've got those times worked out. From the hotel across to Pixy Cove: three minutes. That's walking till you're out of sight of the hotel and then running like mad.
Quicker than I thought.
Down the ladder to the beach: one minute and three-quarters. Climbing back up: two minutes. That's Constable Flint, he's a bit of an athlete. To walk normally from the hotel to the cove via the ladder takes about a quarter of an hour.
What time was the causeway uncovered?
About 9.30, sir.
So who came here? Stalker, blackmailer...
...or drug dealer?

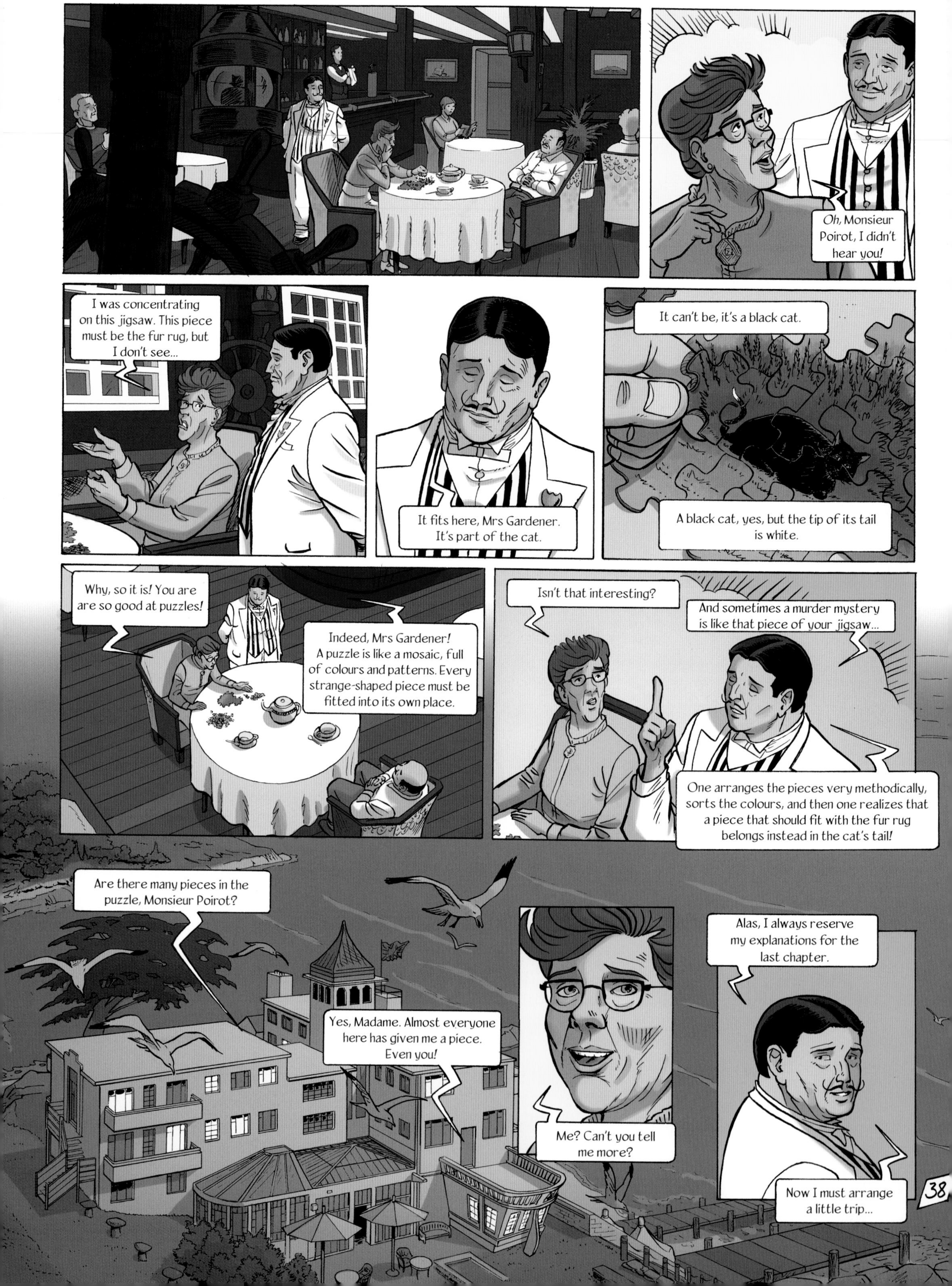

Oh, Monsieur Poirot, I didn't hear you!
I was concentrating on this jigsaw. This piece must be the fur rug, but I don't see...
It fits here, Mrs Gardener. It's part of the cat.
It can't be, it's a black cat.
A black cat, yes, but the tip of its tail is white.
Why, so it is! You are are so good at puzzles!
Indeed, Mrs Gardener! A puzzle is like a mosaic, full of colours and patterns. Every strange-shaped piece must be fitted into its own place.
Isn't that interesting?
And sometimes a murder mystery is like that piece of your jigsaw...
One arranges the pieces very methodically, sorts the colours, and then one realizes that a piece that should fit with the fur rug belongs instead in the cat's tail!
Are there many pieces in the puzzle, Monsieur Poirot?
Yes, Madame. Almost everyone here has given me a piece. Even you!
Me? Can't you tell me more?
Alas, I always reserve my explanations for the last chapter.
Now I must arrange a little trip...

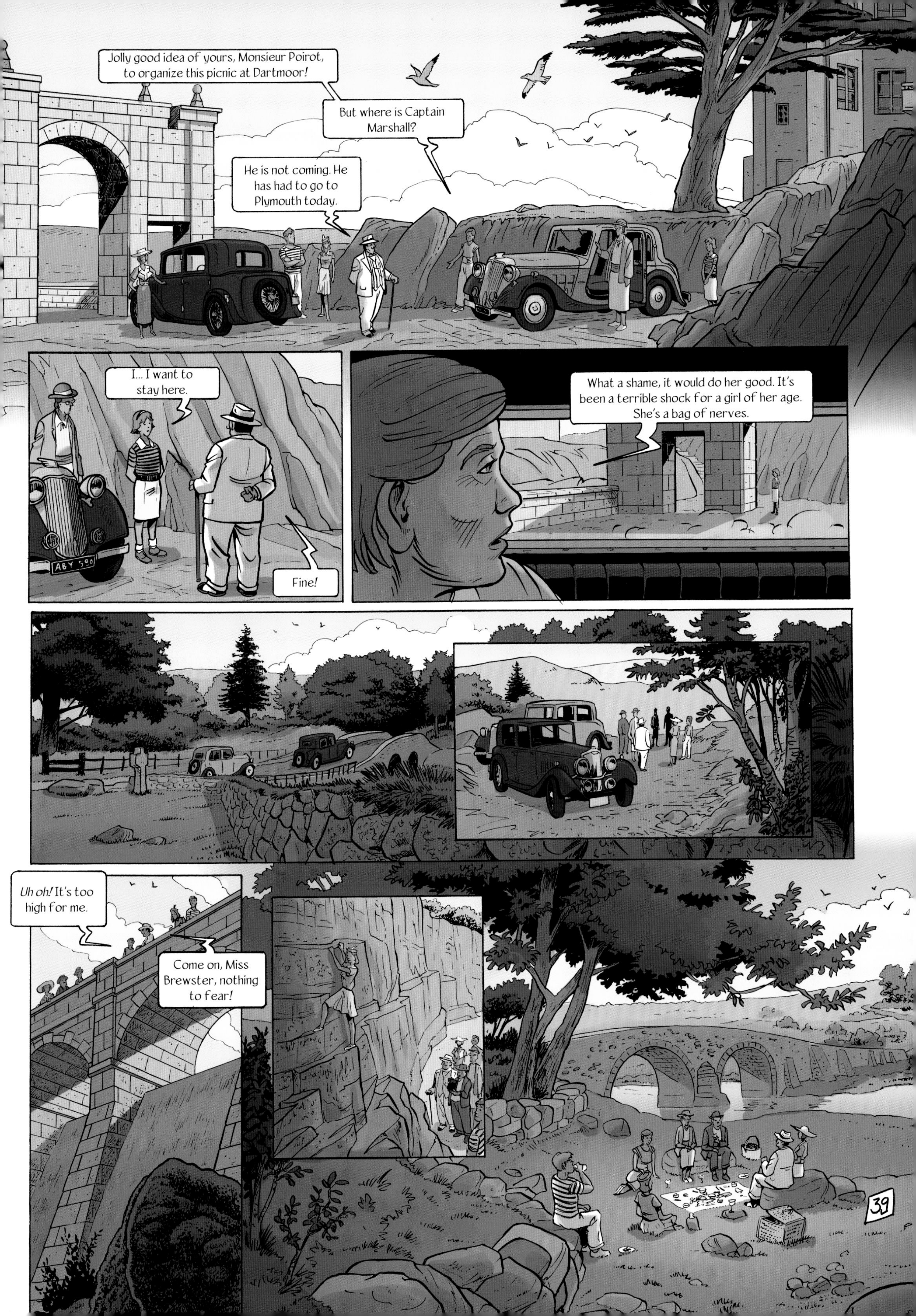
Jolly good idea of yours, Monsieur Poirot, to organize this picnic at Dartmoor!
But where is Captain Marshall?
He is not coming. He has had to go to Plymouth today.
I... I want to stay here.
Fine!
What a shame, it would do her good. It's been a terrible shock for a girl of her age. She's a bag of nerves.
Uh oh! It's too high for me.
Come on, Miss Brewster, nothing to fear!

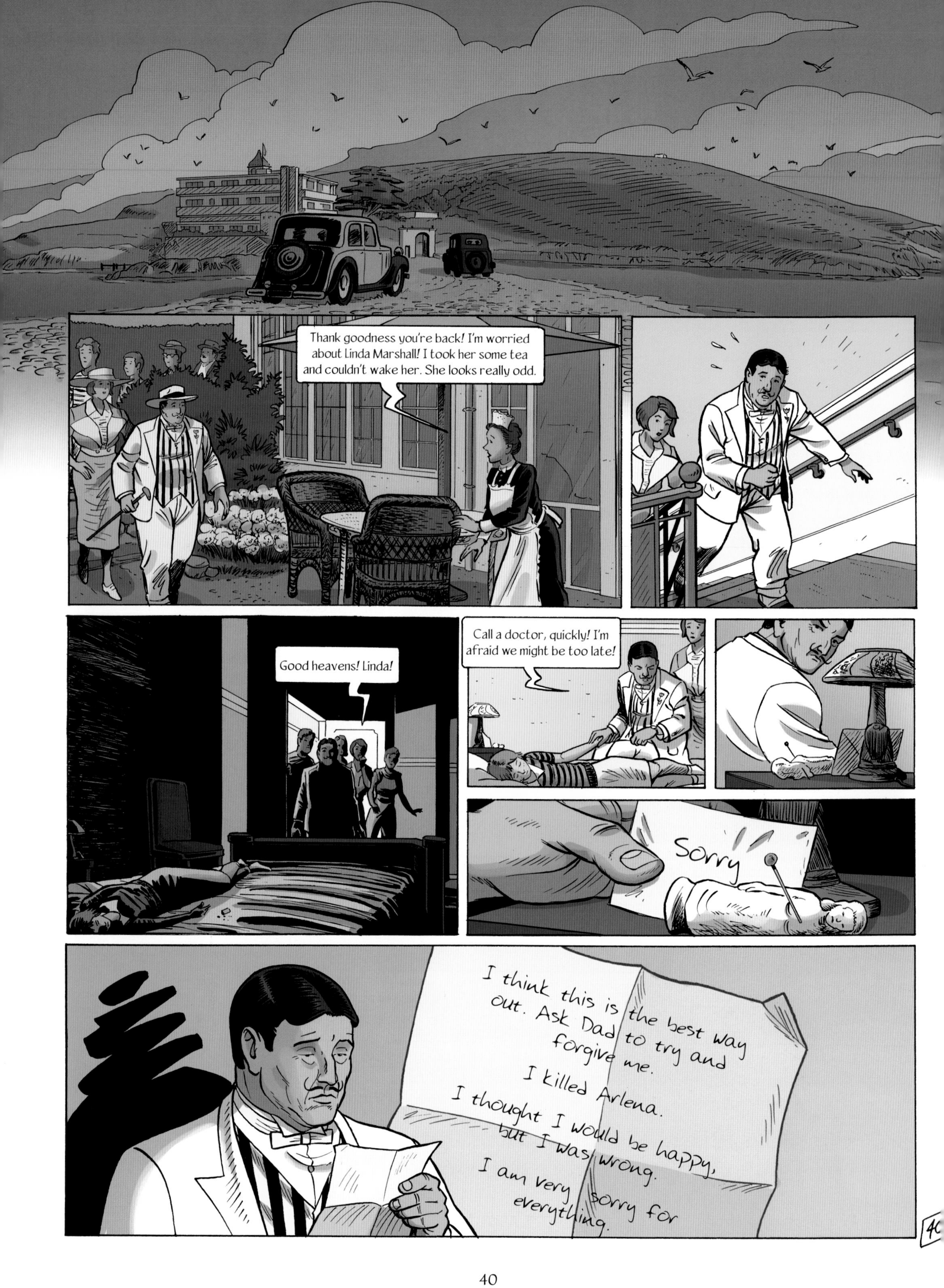
Thank goodness you're back! I'm worried about Linda Marshall! I took her some tea and couldn't wake her. She looks really odd.
Good heavens! Linda!
Call a doctor, quickly! I'm afraid we might be too late!
Sorry
I think this is the best way out. Ask Dad to try and forgive me.
I killed Arlena.
I thought I would be happy, but I was wrong.
I am very sorry for everything.
40

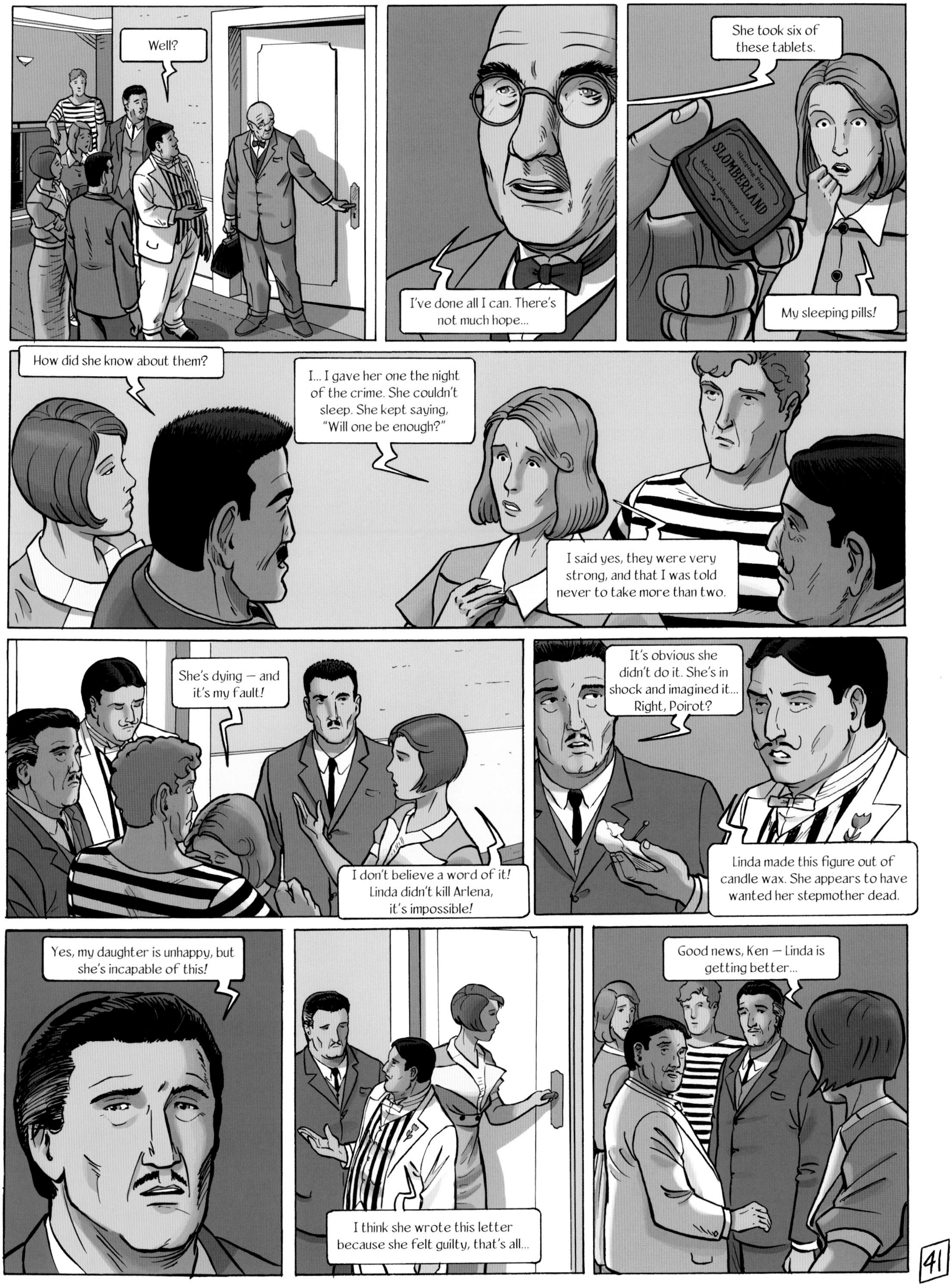
Well?
I've done all I can. There's not much hope...
She took six of these tablets.
Sleeping Pills SLUMBERLAND McCay Laboratory Ltd
My sleeping pills!
How did she know about them?
I... I gave her one the night of the crime. She couldn't sleep. She kept saying, "Will one be enough?"
I said yes, they were very strong, and that I was told never to take more than two.
She's dying — and it's my fault!
I don't believe a word of it! Linda didn't kill Arlena, it's impossible!
It's obvious she didn't do it. She's in shock and imagined it... Right, Poirot?
Linda made this figure out of candle wax. She appears to have wanted her stepmother dead.
Yes, my daughter is unhappy, but she's incapable of this!
I think she wrote this letter because she felt guilty, that's all...
Good news, Ken — Linda is getting better...
41

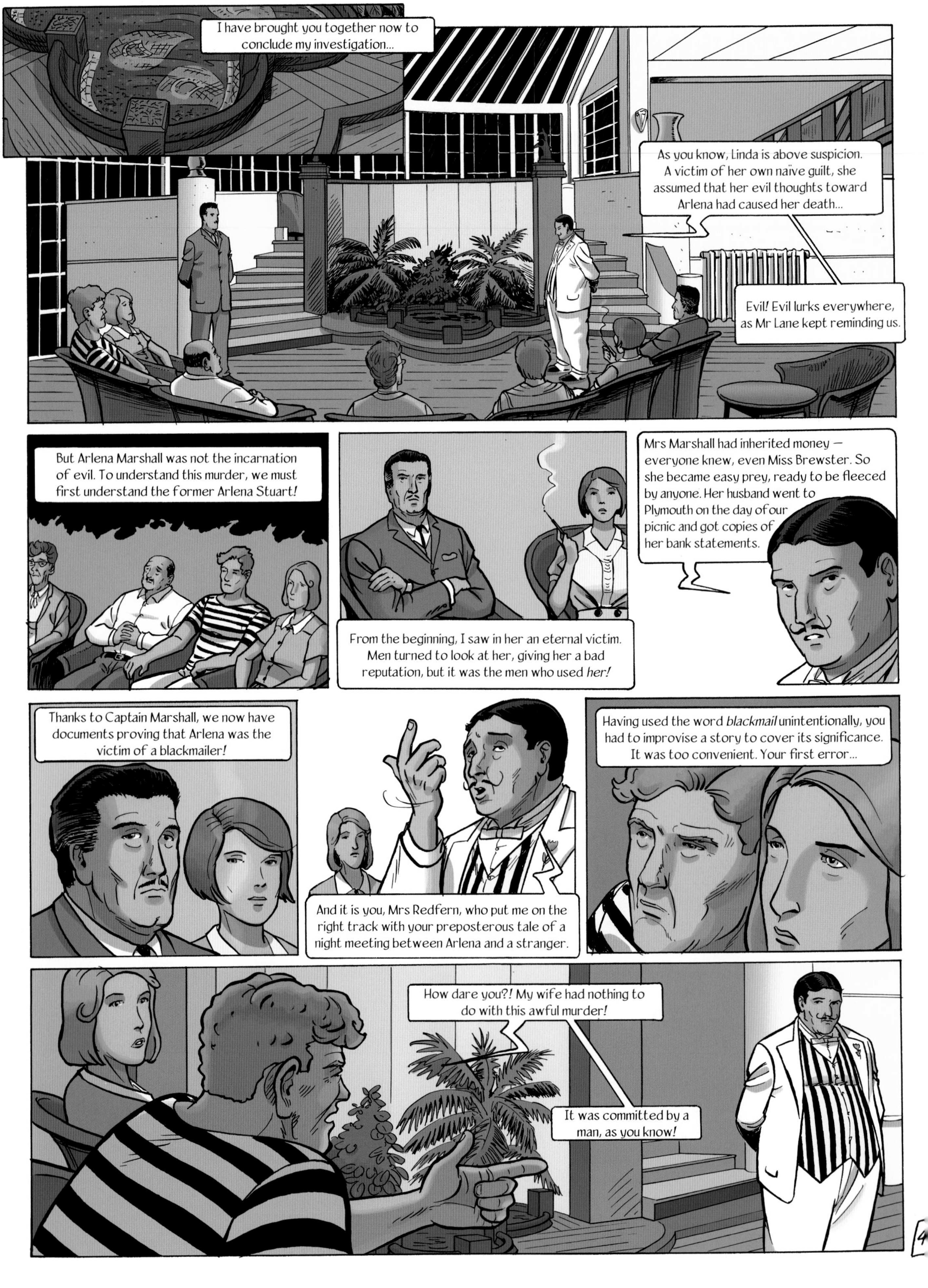

I have brought you together now to conclude my investigation...
As you know, Linda is above suspicion. A victim of her own naïve guilt, she assumed that her evil thoughts toward Arlena had caused her death...
Evil! Evil lurks everywhere, as Mr Lane kept reminding us.
But Arlena Marshall was not the incarnation of evil. To understand this murder, we must first understand the former Arlena Stuart!
From the beginning, I saw in her an eternal victim. Men turned to look at her, giving her a bad reputation, but it was the men who used *her!*
Mrs Marshall had inherited money — everyone knew, even Miss Brewster. So she became easy prey, ready to be fleeced by anyone. Her husband went to Plymouth on the day of our picnic and got copies of her bank statements.
Thanks to Captain Marshall, we now have documents proving that Arlena was the victim of a blackmailer!
And it is you, Mrs Redfern, who put me on the right track with your preposterous tale of a night meeting between Arlena and a stranger.
Having used the word *blackmail* unintentionally, you had to improvise a story to cover its significance. It was too convenient. Your first error...
How dare you?! My wife had nothing to do with this awful murder!
It was committed by a man, as you know!

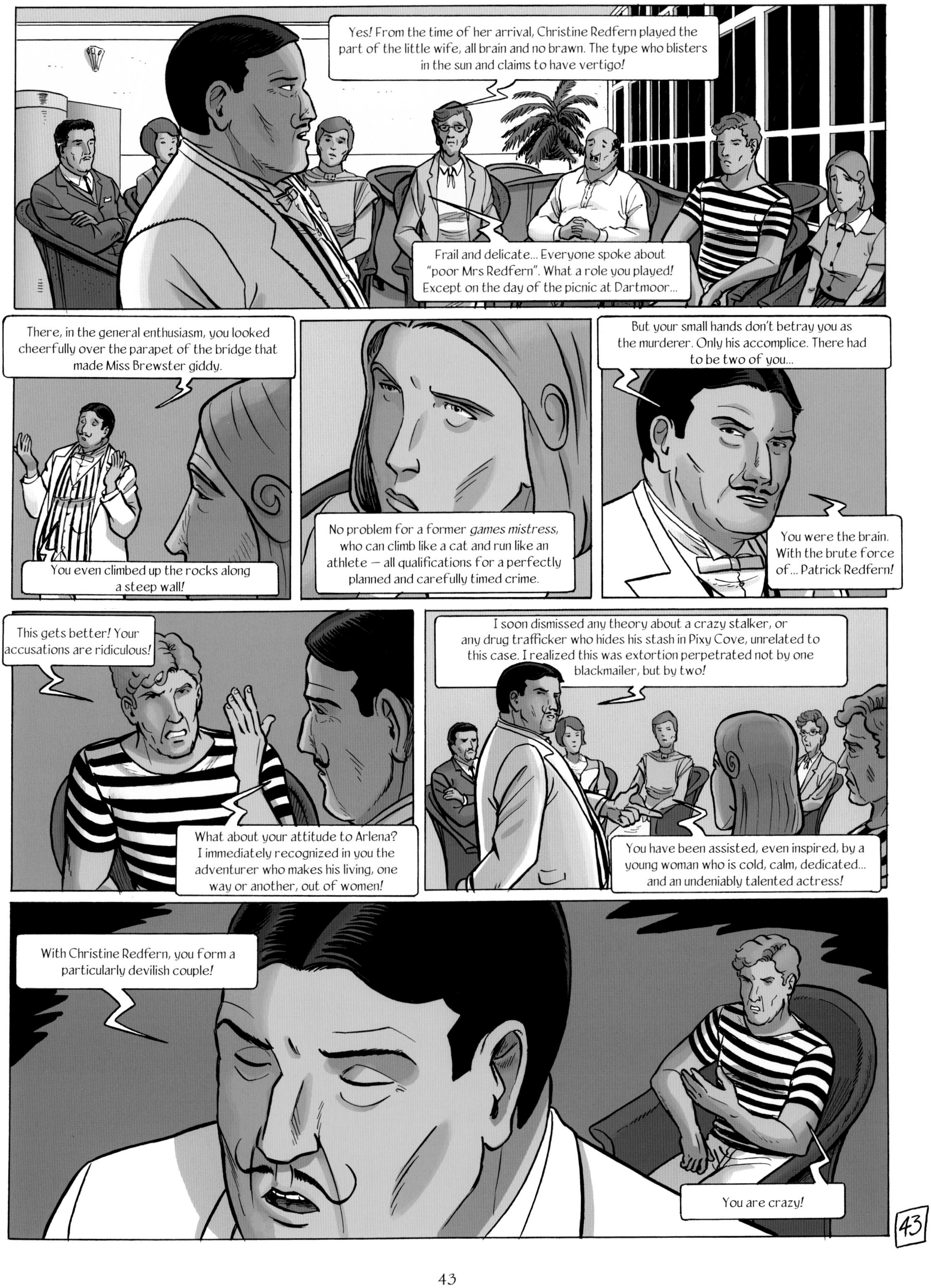
Yes! From the time of her arrival, Christine Redfern played the part of the little wife, all brain and no brawn. The type who blisters in the sun and claims to have vertigo!
Frail and delicate... Everyone spoke about "poor Mrs Redfern". What a role you played! Except on the day of the picnic at Dartmoor...
There, in the general enthusiasm, you looked cheerfully over the parapet of the bridge that made Miss Brewster giddy.
You even climbed up the rocks along a steep wall!
No problem for a former *games mistress*, who can climb like a cat and run like an athlete — all qualifications for a perfectly planned and carefully timed crime.
But your small hands don't betray you as the murderer. Only his accomplice. There had to be two of you...
You were the brain. With the brute force of... Patrick Redfern!
This gets better! Your accusations are ridiculous!
What about your attitude to Arlena? I immediately recognized in you the adventurer who makes his living, one way or another, out of women!
I soon dismissed any theory about a crazy stalker, or any drug trafficker who hides his stash in Pixy Cove, unrelated to this case. I realized this was extortion perpetrated not by one blackmailer, but by two!
You have been assisted, even inspired, by a young woman who is cold, calm, dedicated... and an undeniably talented actress!
With Christine Redfern, you form a particularly devilish couple!
You are crazy!
43

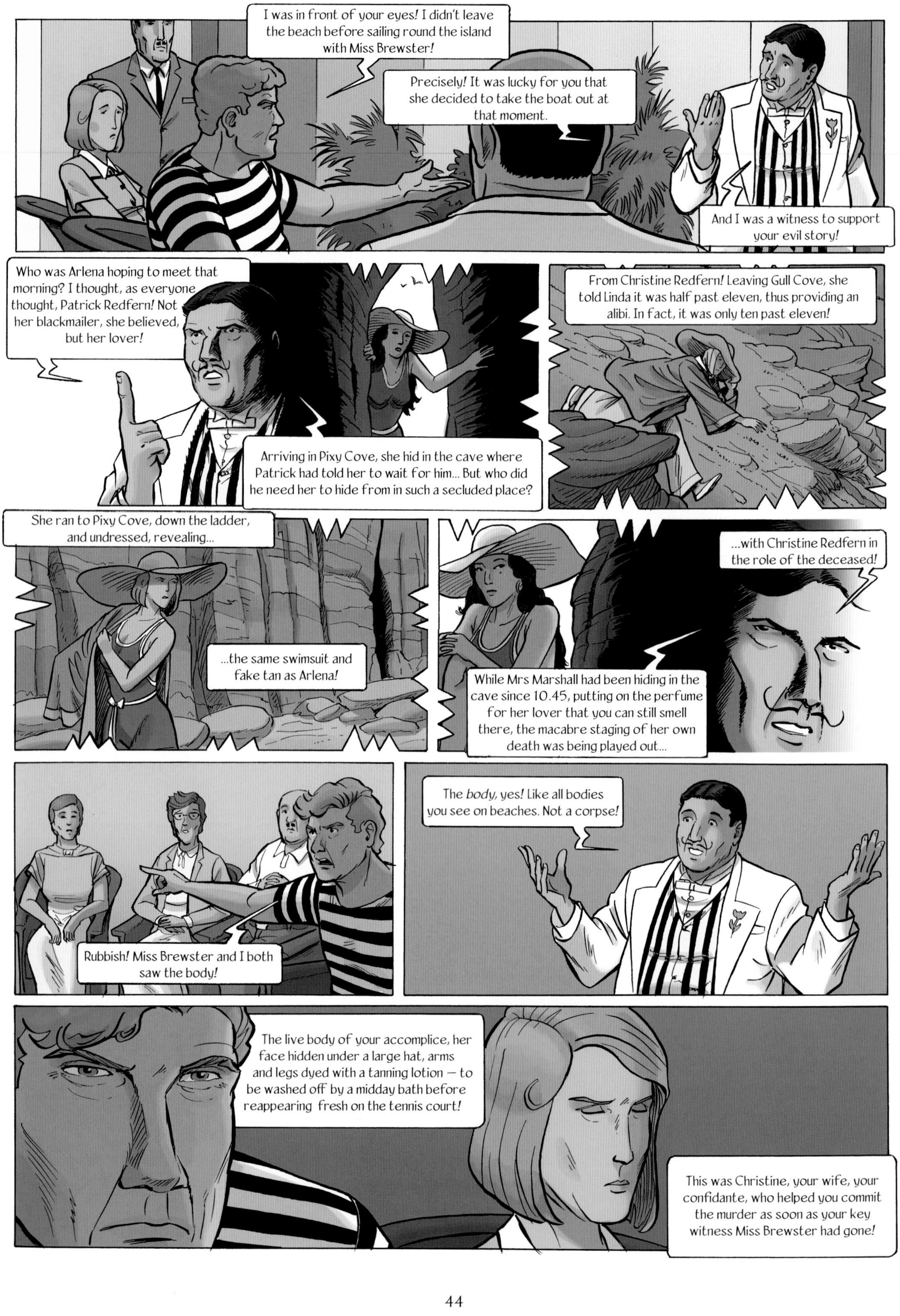

I was in front of your eyes! I didn't leave the beach before sailing round the island with Miss Brewster!
Precisely! It was lucky for you that she decided to take the boat out at that moment.
And I was a witness to support your evil story!
Who was Arlena hoping to meet that morning? I thought, as everyone thought, Patrick Redfern! Not her blackmailer, she believed, but her lover!
Arriving in Pixy Cove, she hid in the cave where Patrick had told her to wait for him... But who did he need her to hide from in such a secluded place?
From Christine Redfern! Leaving Gull Cove, she told Linda it was half past eleven, thus providing an alibi. In fact, it was only ten past eleven!
She ran to Pixy Cove, down the ladder, and undressed, revealing...
...the same swimsuit and fake tan as Arlena!
...with Christine Redfern in the role of the deceased!
While Mrs Marshall had been hiding in the cave since 10.45, putting on the perfume for her lover that you can still smell there, the macabre staging of her own death was being played out...
Rubbish! Miss Brewster and I both saw the body!
The *body*, yes! Like all bodies you see on beaches. Not a corpse!
The live body of your accomplice, her face hidden under a large hat, arms and legs dyed with a tanning lotion — to be washed off by a midday bath before reappearing fresh on the tennis court!
This was Christine, your wife, your confidante, who helped you commit the murder as soon as your key witness Miss Brewster had gone!

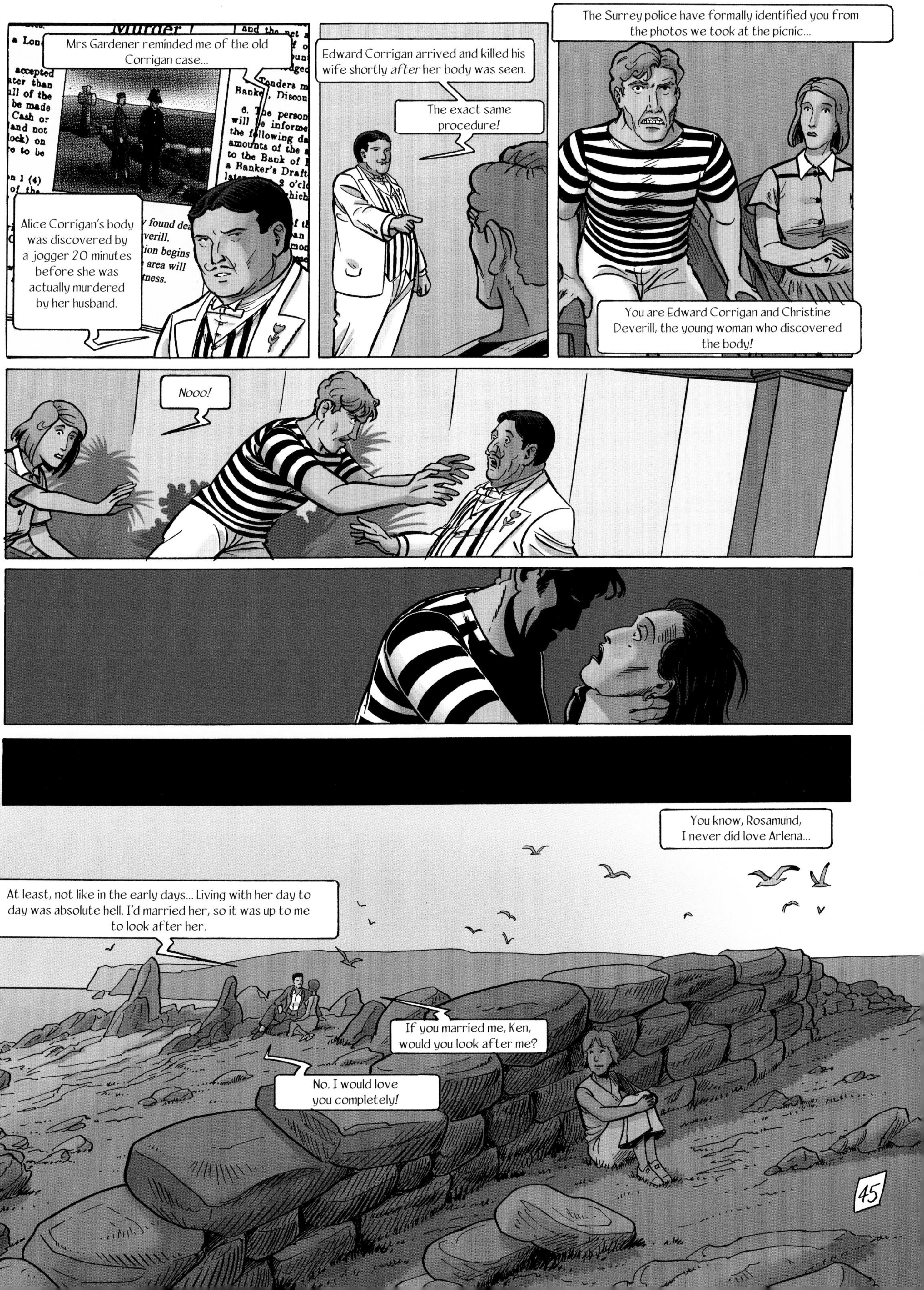

Mrs Gardener reminded me of the old Corrigan case...
Alice Corrigan's body was discovered by a jogger 20 minutes before she was actually murdered by her husband.
Edward Corrigan arrived and killed his wife shortly *after* her body was seen.
The exact same procedure!
The Surrey police have formally identified you from the photos we took at the picnic...
You are Edward Corrigan and Christine Deverill, the young woman who discovered the body!
Nooo!
You know, Rosamund, I never did love Arlena...
At least, not like in the early days... Living with her day to day was absolute hell. I'd married her, so it was up to me to look after her.
If you married me, Ken, would you look after me?
No. I would love you completely!

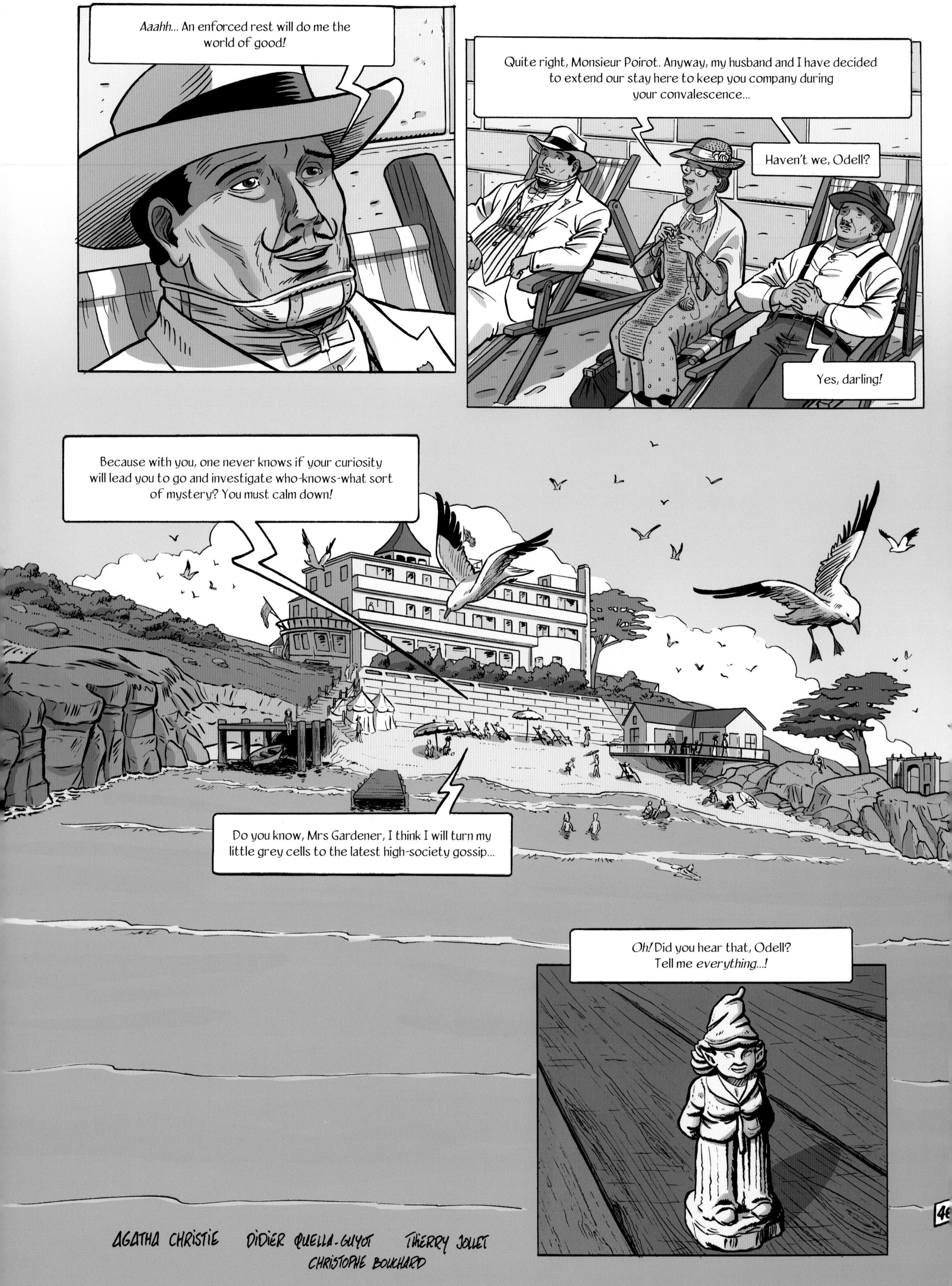
Aaahh... An enforced rest will do me the world of good!
Quite right, Monsieur Poirot. Anyway, my husband and I have decided to extend our stay here to keep you company during your convalescence...
Haven't we, Odell?
Yes, darling!
Because with you, one never knows if your curiosity will lead you to go and investigate who-knows-what sort of mystery? You must calm down!
Do you know, Mrs Gardener, I think I will turn my little grey cells to the latest high-society gossip...
Oh! Did you hear that, Odell? Tell me everything...!
AGATHA CHRISTIE DIDIER QUELLA-GUYOT THIERRY JOLLET
CHRISTOPHE BOUCHARD